Love is Complicated

A Romance Anthology

LUW Romance Chapter

Love is Complicated
A Romance Anthology

Contents

Introduction

Love is Complicated, that's why we love romance. It's not always certain but it's wondrous when it happens.
Here at the League of Utah Writers Romance Chapter, we believe in happily ever afters in this complicated world, and we are delighted to share these stories with you. From members and non members alike. We all share a common theme, love is worth it.

Melissa Schack, Co-President
Keyra K. Allred, Co-President

Pedestal

Alex Child

Silly me
I gave you that pedestal
To help you reach
The birds and the sky and the sun
But all it did
Was force you
To look down on me

The Trumpington Bride

Virginia Babcock

I dreamt of her again. The news story showing her simulated face haunts me. They got it wrong, so wrong. But only I am left alive to know. My Hilda has been dead for more than 1,300 years, but my heart still yearns for her. My collections always contain garnets in gold in her honor. I pray one day I can die and finally join her in heaven.

***

Lord Chad held his new bride, Hilda close. Their chamber was the only walled off room in the great hall of the keep, and was the main reason he'd chosen this fortified town of Whitesford as his primary residence. If he'd remained in his father's castle, they'd be relegated to one of the unheated side chambers near his honored mother's ladies. Besides, his father was old, and soon enough, he'd own that keep to have and hold upon his father's demise. Also, what was another holding? His father was lord over sufficient keeps and towns to satisfy the needs of all six of his sons.

Whitesford was a rich village well protected by the fortified castle on the high hill overlooking its mill and quarry. Here, dense forests surrounded lush fields and prosperous holds. Chad's new lady's dower funds would fill the stores with spices and rich furnishings. Already her father had sent a dozen fine-bred colts for his knights to train and ride, along with a fat sow and her piglets to strengthen his herds. With the bountiful harvests of wheat, millet, and barley, this winter should be full of plenty. And his people would be able to try eating more meat and cheese as his wife preferred.

Marrying during the fall festival allowed he and his lady to hold a three-day celebration feast for their families and distinguished guests. It had also allowed them a last adventure to the river bend for some water play before the river froze. Hilda had never done more than wade in the springs of her faraway, mountain home. But Chad's mother had grown up along the seashore. His father's older brother had drowned as a boy, so his mother had taught all her children to swim at a young age.

After their first week together Chad's new lady's hair still shone with cleanliness and her skin was the creamy pink of milk loaded with berries once the berries were eaten. He picked up the long strand covering her breast that was draped over a shapely hip. It was the rich brown of well-turned earth, but shone like the golden coins and garnets her mother had gifted her upon her twelfth birthday.

They should have married then, but a fever struck the land that spring. It took another two seasons for his family's lands, people, and flocks to recover. Now three years later, some wondered if his bride was too old. But to him, she was lushly formed. Her hips were wide and well padded. Her ankles and wrists were trim and daintily curved. And she had survived the fevers well, so her luscious locks were never cut and reached her knees when unbound.

They had enjoyed well the pleasures of the wedding bed, and nightly he prayed she would soon be seeded with his firstborn son. The priest had promised it. The wood witch who followed the old gods gave her raspberry leaves in a potion to guarantee it.

His moving of her long locks awoke his bride. She smiled at him and caressed his cheek. He kissed her soft lips and offered her wine from the skin atop the nearby coffer. Together they finished the sweet vintage. He ran a finger from the bottom of her ear to her collarbone. In response she hooked a limber leg over his side and slid closer. He playfully growled against her neck and pulled her tight against him, pressing his chest into her soft breasts. They missed the nightly meal once again.

* * *

My lady love spent the winter in comfort. My seed took. Her courses never came from the time we were wedded. The weight of our child rides well, brightens Hilda's eyes, and has added a pleasant fullness to her womanhood. Even in these lean times as winter fights the coming of spring, she is joyful and kind. Plus, her wood lore from her home across the sea has benefited our tribes. She has healed many a hurt and eased most sickness.

Her two ladies in waiting have arrived. Each has made a good marriage to one of my men at arms, and they too are increasing. My father sent word that my own mother is also expecting again. She has borne him twelve babes in excellent health and expects that this final babe will be gifted and lucky as its birth order and due date will match the old gods' benevolent thirteenth month. Once again both our Christian priest and our Pagan mother have taken credit for our fecundity.

* * *

On Midsummer's Day of the year following my marriage, my life was full. We had celebrated the Lord's death and rebirth, and were preparing to celebrate the Goddesses Day. My son was three months old, and was often found in my arms as I did my daily tasks. My daughter was often with her mother due to her active energy. Hilda, my lady wife had been blessed with twins.

My son was born first and feet first. His birth was difficult and only his small size enabled him and my wife to survive. Our daughter arrived soon after him, in perfect position and screaming with displeasure. She was half a finger's length longer and almost a pound heavier.

My wife and the wood mother advised me that my son needs much rest and easy nourishment. As I suffered a sword wound in the midwinter tourney, I have less to do this season and enjoy carrying him around. His wet nurse is in constant attendance and the boy is gaining ground in line with my own healing.

Another maypole has been erected. Flock firstlings that survived the Lord's feast are on great spits. Early fruits and vegetables are laid out on large tables along with fresh baked goods and new cheese. Vats of last fall's ales and aged vintages have been rolled out from the cellars and rest ready for their breaching. Warriors and youngsters race and play at mock battles. Maids are chased by their swains as prospective couples scout a nest in which to spend the year's shortest night.

My own wife has arranged for her ladies to care for our children so that we may play at love ourselves when the twilight comes. I've formed a cozy nest in the tall grasses below the crook of a mighty oak and lined it with bed linens. This eve I hope to plant my seed firmly once again.

At midday the dances start. My wife leads the young virgins to the maypole and begins their dance. As the streamers weave, she looks my way and smiles. She seems as young and free as the girls surrounding her.

The day progresses. I award the winners of the various games with trinkets and bits of silver. My wife hands out lengths of ribbon and garlands of flowers. The feasting begins at midafternoon and will continue until the food is gone. When darkness falls, we slip away to our forest hideaway. We are not the first couple to wander off, nor will we be the last.

In the twilight, my wife and I renew our love again and again. Moonrise finds us entwined. I lay on Hilda's chest as she braids the ends of her hair. Our lovemaking had loosened the two long coils from her head. I listen to her heart as my cheek relishes the warmth of her skin. Earlier I had eased the milk from her weighted breasts and we had played in the nearby creek to cool off. The air is crisp and fragrant with the smell of freshly crushed grass and rich earth from the roots beneath us.

Suddenly, a loud noise of thunder sounds. The sky turns gloomy as clouds hide the moon. Heavy rain pelts us as I try to cover my lady with our bedding. Sheets of cold water soak us. Another flash of lightning follows with thunder accompanying it directly overhead. A new shower of sparks rain down as the mighty oak suffers the strike of heaven's fire. Pain shoots through my body. The world turns to a black void.

I wake sometime later. It must be morning, because it's no longer dark. A blue mist surrounds us. I also smell woodsmoke. My teeth chatter. I'm freezing. I look for my wife. I can't find her warmth. I stand and take two steps. I trip over the tangled bedding and land on something cold and hard.

My wife is dead.

Her body is stiff and cold. Her eyes are sightless and open. A charred hole rides high on her forehead. I check her limbs and body and find no other damage but a smaller burnt wound in her left foot above her toe. A blackened spot in the grass lies near her feet.

I look upward, straining to see the sky. I beg my Lord, my God to wake me up as if this were a dream. I see the mighty oak burning instead. It's split into two halves from its top to its roots that smolder in front of my face. The rain has put out its fire, and I remember.

The bright light of the lightning blinded me as it struck the oak and traveled down to where we lay at its base. The blow threw me out away from the tree, but the white fire must have traveled through my beloved, killing her with its heat.

Voices call through the mist. The wood witch leads the group. They search for us and for others caught in the storm. They find me first. My steward helps me dress as the mother wraps my wife in a sheet. They support me as I carry Hilda back to our home. On the way, the priestess describes the awful portents she read in the surprise storm. It lasted three days. My wife was not its lone casualty. The splitting of the great oak confirms the signs. The old gods were displeased.

In the chapel, the priest blesses me as I place my beloved on the altar. His words bring no comfort. Our Christian God was little protection from the primal storm. A dozen others lost their lives as well. Some through drowning as the surprise rains caused the river and its tributaries to overflow their banks. Others were lost from cold as the wind and rains found their hiding places. Two holds burned when lightning struck them. The dead were cleaned and prepared; and also laid out in the timbered church.

We bury the common folk first in the blessed ground of the churchyard. My wife receives pride of place. Our children cry as her grave is dug. I lay the fine bedframe with its fresh tick on the ropes myself. My wife's ladies drape her final bed in the softest linen, and then back away. I lay her down and observe her ladies straighten her hem and sleeves and arrange her veil with its golden chain and pins over her hair. I pull the end of her chatelaine to flow down her legs and fold her arms across her chest. Her favorite gown covers her in dark red over the warm ivory of her chemise. I pin her most prized possession, her golden cross encrusted with garnets, to her veil above her heart. The rest of her gold and garnet jewelry will go to our daughter. Her lengthy braids rest heavy by her sides.

My strongest men move forward and lift the grave bed on its ropes. Gently they shuffle to her burial hole and lower her down. Once the earth covers her I turn away and retreat to the keep. Ale, mead, and wine become my boon companions.

* * *

I spent nearly a month insensible with grief. Finally, the priest and my knights captured me and held me prisoner in the smithy until I became sober. They chained me to the anvil until I stopped raving. Eventually they devised a schedule to bring me back to myself. Each day the smith would douse me awake with a bucket of water warmed by his hearth. Gruel was my only meat. New wine my only drink. Eventually I regained my senses.

My men protected my lands and did my duties during this time. My wife's ladies took care of my children. The priest and mother made daily visits to gauge my madness. Eventually I understood that I must decide to live or choose to die. I chose life.

I raised my first-born twins. I even remarried and had more children. Eventually my lands increased as did my prosperity.

Now and then I would return to Whitesford to visit my wife's grave. Over the years I learned that I was afflicted in some way. Those struck by the gods' fire were supposed to die. I had been struck while holding my wife but only she died. Then the priestess mother informed me that I would not die until she, my wife, lived again. That was my curse.

At first I didn't believe her. But on my fortieth birthday, my men took to teasing me. They had aged, but I still looked young. On my fiftieth birthday, I began covering my still dark and full hair and bleaching my beard to appear older. As my sons began looking older than myself I knew I had to leave.

The mother, then very aged, helped me go. She taught me her ways and I became a wise man and a wanderer. My wife's gold coins and garnets were also cursed. I would spend them or give them away, but the next day, they returned to my pouch. With this knowledge and afflicted wealth, I've survived to this day.

Through the ages, my name and occupation have changed as have my alliances, to suit the times. My face and frame have not. I remain the strong man of twenty or so seasons who was once chief of all he surveyed. Every generation or so I kill myself and inherit my sustained and accumulated wealth before moving to a new place.

A century or two after my cursing, I had become a hermit and a mystic. People sought me for spells and wisdom. I gave them natural cures and sound advice. Eventually they termed me a wizard. I became Merlin. And the fact that I could not save Arthur proved to me that I was still only a man. A cursed, doomed man.

I stayed in what most now call England for hundreds of years. I've also lived everywhere else in the world. But for the last few hundred years I made my home in America. I chose this place, because the bulk of my descendants came to the colonies when the English invaded these shores. By working with Benjamin Franklin, I learned how the lightning killed Hilda. Later I saw images of wounds caused by that infernal phenomena. I know now that it entered her body through her head and left through her foot.

Like the mother, the priest agreed that I was cursed, but explained it was due to my "bad" actions; though he could give me no examples of such. He claimed the three days I lay as if dead mimicked the Lord's death. He advised me to follow Christ's teachings and serve others. I believe now that I will die when my wife lives, which means I will live until the end of days, when Christ returns.

I tried living both goodly and evilly. Neither way helped nor hindered me. But for the past millennium, I've tried to live doing good. There's simply too much bad in the world. I don't want to add more evil. I've also learned my own needs. I better enjoy my days when I can take pride in my actions. I stay busy by creating things and helping others. My latest occupation is jewelry designer.

Just over ten years ago I felt a change. The days became sharper and I felt happiness reenter my life. I had done nothing different, nor met anyone new. As this continued for a few months I learned the cause. Archeologists had found my wife's grave and dug her up.

So few burials from my natal time survived that her grave is rewriting history. As for me, I can view her bones and the bits of metal and jewelry that outlasted her flesh. Her cross, what they call the Trumpington Cross, named after my ancestral lands, is now famous and far away from its rightful place upon her breast.

How the sight of her skull hurts my heart. What I wouldn't give to be reduced to a skeleton or dust with her. She's in a box or a drawer when not on display, and this pains me too. They've inventoried her corporeal remains by numbering them. I should have burned her like my Pagan forebears burned their dead.

In the last few days, they've "recreated" Hilda's face. I see it feeling both joy and sorrow. It's a close likeness, though her eyes were blue. The image doesn't show her full beauty. But what I miss most is her glory, her hair. The artist made it short and held close to her head. But, when loose under her circlet and veil it rode in great, wavy curves. Her hair floated away from her scalp even when pulled tightly. Her eyelashes were dark, long, and full. Her skin was pink and rosy, not sallow and washed out.

Their data is otherwise correct. We were betrothed nearly 600 years after the lord's birth, and she was raised in the high mountains of Europe in what is now part of

Germany. She migrated to join my family at age twelve and died just before her seventeenth birthday. Modern humans don't think pre-medieval humans migrated so far. I long to tell the truths of my time. Yet I cannot.

I think often of the Lord's Beloved apostle and wonder at the sights he's seen since his passing into immortality. The discovery of Hilda's remains has renewed my faith. I pray every day for relief or a solution. I beg the Lord to release me from this world or return her to it.

* * *

BREAKING NEWS
Trumpington Cross Stolen

CAMBRIDGE, England — Famed jeweler Chadwick Whitesford is wanted by British Authorities for allegedly stealing the Trumpington Grave's occupant and jewels, including the famous Trumpington Cross, from their display at the Cambridge University Museum.

The renowned artist had been hired by museum officials to create replica jewelry to sell in their stores. While inspecting the actual pieces, Whitesford requested to view the female remains in order to "get an impression of the woman who wore the jewelry."

Authorities did not provide any further details beyond claiming Whitesford absconded with everything from the grave and should be considered extremely dangerous. We've received unsubstantiated reports that Whitesford used a replica sword from the same Anglo-Saxon era to cut down the staff guarding these priceless artifacts.

FBI and Interpol personnel were seen investigating Whitesford's New England mansion. In response to our requests for more information, law enforcement representatives stated they do not comment on active investigations.

* * *

A well-preserved Norman church has taken the place of Whitesford keep. I made it this far, because the museum staff couldn't conceive I would rescue Hilda and her jewelry. Also, I know the area better than anyone, though it's now called Whittlesford. The cellar under the church used to house the remains of some of our children's great-great-grandchildren.

I have her gold and garnets along with sufficient petrol. A storm is coming. I will be with my beloved forever.

* * *

****BREAKING NEWS****
Priceless Treasures Lost

WHITTLESFORD, England — Local authorities have identified the person whose remains were found in the ruins of St. Andrews church as Chadwick Whitesford of Boston, Massachusetts, USA. They confirm on the night that lightning struck the church, Whitesford was already in the area below the altar having doused the chapel with an accelerant. His actions caused the fire that destroyed the church.

Cambridge University Museum officials also confirmed that the remains of the Trumpington Anglo-Saxon lady and her grave goods, including her jewelry and the Trumpington Cross were destroyed in the fire and resulting collapse of the 11th century structure. Officials from multiple agencies all agree that the loss of the priceless grave goods and the ancient church is horrific.

It's unknown whether Whitesford had intended to die in the church or whether the lightning ignited his fuel before he could escape.

* * *

Cambridge Daily Gossiper
Trumpington Lady Found?

Mysteriously, the Trumpington Lady's gold and garnet hair chain has been found. It was returned to the Cambridge University Museum without fanfare or explanation last week.

An anonymous source has come forward blaming an unnamed Cambridge University Museum official for the fire that destroyed the St. Andrews church in Whittlesford last year. The purported motive was to frame the still missing Chadwick Whitesford for the Trumpington grave theft.

Our source maintains that no human remains were actually found in the destroyed church. Our sources have confirmed the original burials were transferred to the churchyard in the 19th century after a flood. Despite official reports, we could locate no human remains of any kind recovered from the church in police or museum custody.

Rumor suggests the unnamed culprit and/or thief apparently returned the veil chain to the museum out of guilt. Meanwhile, there is no sign of the Trumpington Lady herself, or her famous gold and garnet cross. US authorities confirm Chadwick has not returned to his home or work, and remains on their Most Wanted list.

Interestingly, a portion of the insurance settlement proceeds has gone missing. Locals suspect a conspiracy. Was Chadwick in cahoots with the museum employee? Will we ever get our Anglo-Saxon teenager back? All of Cambridge wants to know.

Be sure to subscribe for more information.

Tell Me Something

Elizabeth Suggs

"Tell me something," I whispered, running my hands down Trevor's naked backside as we lay in his bed.

It was late, probably near four in the morning. I should have gone to sleep. I needed to leave for the airport early tomorrow morning, but I couldn't close my eyes.

"Tell you something?" he asked, fatigue of our recent activities pulling down his eyes.

This was a game I liked to play with him, one that filled the silence and also told me what he was thinking about.

He took me into his arms and held me close. "Well, I know that I love you, and whenever we're together, I never want to be anywhere else."

"How are you going to cope when I move?" It was a question constantly on my mind, especially now that my leave was near. I tried not to ask him much, but sometimes, like right now, the words burst out of me.

"I'll still think about you, and wish you were close, but you'll be back soon."

"Three years soon," I said softly, as if he didn't already know, as if I didn't have it plastered over all our calendars and mention it to anyone in passing.

The three-year contract was an expedition to Antarctica to research the effects of how quickly the glaciers were actually melting.

I never expected to be on something like this. Most of my research had been in university labs or going for weekend conferences, helping to dispel the misbeliefs of climate change. I could have been perfectly happy doing that for the rest of my life—living with Trevor and maybe getting a cat. But when my colleague suggested the trip, explained the opportunity, I knew I would be a fool to pass it up, even if I could barely stand our 30-degree winters.

Trevor had been surprisingly supportive, which only made it worse. Maybe if he had raged—threatened to destroy the relationship, I'd've felt better about leaving, but instead he had helped pack my things and get me the most effective winter gear.

"Three years is a long time, though. What if another woman breaks your new guitar, and you fall madly in love with her?"

"You know I wouldn't do that." He kissed me softly. I'd miss those kisses. "Besides, no one is as clumsy as you."

I pushed him back playfully, feigning anger. "It was not clumsiness! A drunk guy pushed me into you!"

"Uh-huh, likely story," he said with a wry smile. He kissed the top of my freckled shoulder.

We met five years ago after one of his performances. He'd been playing a one-man show, bouncing between drums and guitar. Usually, I only half-watched the performances as most of my attention centered around my research and my Belgium ale, but I couldn't keep my eyes off him—the electricity in which he moved between his instruments had me transfixed.

And when I went up to him to compliment his performance, a half-conscious man plowed into me, causing me to fall into Trevor and his guitar.

"I paid for the repairs," I said.

"I told you you didn't have to."

"How else would I have gotten your number?" I said with a smile.

He laughed. "There were other, much easier, ways to get my number."

"Too bad I didn't think about any of those things back then," I said.

He kissed me longer, and we fell into each other, moving in time to that ancient rhythm. When we reemerged, the early morning light peeked through the blinds. Soon, I'd need to be in a taxi, heading to the airport.

Then, Trevor whispered, "Tell me something."

"I don't think I've ever loved someone as deeply as I have loved you," I said.

"That's why I know we can withstand this distance," he said. "Because I love you too. With every fiber of my being. I will wait for you because you're worth waiting for."

Relax

Sara Violet Scully

They always tell me to relax, to be chill. But I had never—not once—released the tension in my love. It remained tightly wound and bound like wrists at the hands of an accidentally casual, kinky lover.

I had a habit of clinging to tenderness, like the nights after Christmas where I was so desired when I was so lonely that I mistook tenderness for love. Thousands of miles from home, on an emerald shore, held in the arms of a man that was both nothing and everything like my ex-husband. He was rougher in every sense of the word, from his grizzled beard, to his demanding touch, to the sharp edges of his criticism. And I didn't just tolerate it. I wanted it. I craved the violent nature of our connection because at least then it was warmed by flames.

From the moment we met, his hands found me, pulling to him—or maybe I just gravitated on my own, my love a satellite falling from the sky with a distress beacon screaming for interception. I fell into his ravaging kiss and stumbled to my lumpy bed, where I experienced true desire for the very first time. Gnawing, clawing, licking, sucking—all the things I had built up in my fantasies made carnal.

And then I cried.

I hate myself for it, because my little satellite heart crashed upon his hairy chest and shattered into messy shards of tears, weeping from the catharsis while thinking somehow my distress call had been answered.

But that was before he cut contact. The last correspondence being one word: *Relax*.

How can one relax their grip when everyone they've ever loved slipped through their fingers? I kept searching for reciprocity, and when I finally found it, I was so terrified that I let go. And then my hands were too tired to reach for love again. Despite my best efforts, I chilled out and became everything that I detested: passive, disingenuous, and cold.

By the time my former lover came back to me, I was too dead inside to desire him. The passion that propelled me before was no longer there. And passion isn't something I can pretend.

The words that lured me before were revealed to me as nothing but an old picnic left for insects to devour. The sustenance I craved was simply leftover scraps, and when the rosy veil was lifted from my eyes, all I could see was a heaping pile of trash. And I ate it anyway. Anything to numb the dull hunger that was once insatiable.

Relax, they say.

Because it's easier to be satisfied when your love has limits.

Uncertain Affections

Mae Thorn

The train click-clapped on its way into Havenville station. The aspens shook at the force of the steel contraption as it blocked the sun from Lena's view. Today would be the day she would welcome home Victor. It had to be.

Dozens of women's shadowed faces smiled despite the chances. It had been months since the last train came in from fighting the Nazis and few had made the journey back home. Many more flags than welcoming hugs were passed around. Too much was taken from Havenville, and only so much love could hold the town together.

Lena scanned the papers every morning, hoping and worrying she would see Victor's name among the soldiers. Her heart squeezed with every appearance of a 'V' and released when a Valentino or Vincent came into view.

Her nerves sizzled and sparked every morning, and by noon, she was a restless creature confined to her home without news. No letters arrived from the front, and no men appeared holding flags. Not for Lena.

Nobody had known about their courtship. Lena was a proper lady, born and bred to marry her merchant father's prodigy, Benjamin, but Lena had other ideas. She had dashed her senses when she met Victor. The kind of man who could fix anything, but also, the type of man who spoke three languages and refused to fight without a cause.

His sleek black hair and generous smile held a familiarity she couldn't place. On that first meeting, she slipped into the Lena nobody knew. The Lena she hid behind her flashy grin and pale pink nails.

Her stomach had lodged in her throat when he had told her about enlisting. Her life seemed to shift and bend at the news. Not Victor. What if she never saw him again? Her world fell away, leaving only the concern for his safety.

The train hissed as it came to a stop, and Lena rose on tiptoes to inspect the windows. Reflections hid the identities of the passengers like a present wrapped under the Christmas tree. Her heart took up the beat of her steps as she raced to the opening doors.

A woman with a child on her hip screeched and ran into the open arms of a man. He huffed as the woman struck him, and the child cried out for his father. The woman erupted in sobs, echoing her son.

Lena stared at the family unit, and she forced her lips to pull up. Victor would be there, and they could start their life together. Never mind what her parents thought. She wouldn't be separated from him for another minute.

"Lena," a familiar voice yelled.

Eugene weaved past the forming couples and enveloped her in his burly arms. "I'm so happy to see you." His teeth gleamed against his olive features.

"I'm happy you made it home." She squeezed back, but she swallowed her tears. Had Victor been delayed? Killed in action? Injured? Her thoughts raced and twisted as she studied her lover's closest friend for answers.

Lena glanced behind Eugene and glanced again.

"Are you sure you're happy to see me?" A gleam lit in his eyes.

She cleared her throat. "Of course."

He chuckled. "I know I'm not Victor."

"Where is he?" Her voice came out a whisper.

Eugene's face lengthened and he studied her. "I didn't want to be the one to tell you this."

Her jaw wobbled and ice wound its way around her chest. "Spit it out."

He let out a heavy sigh. "He's gone."

"Gone?"

"To get his luggage." He erupted in laughter and slapped her on the back.

She stared at him, numb.

A hand gripped her shoulder and she memorized the feel of his capable fingers. She dared not move or the hand might disappear, show itself for the illusion it must be. She blinked, but the hand remained.

"That was a cruel joke, Eugene." His rich baritone ignited goosebumps on her arms.

"Victor… you came back."

He spun her around as though they were on the dance floor again. Two people experiencing a music that only played for them.

Her breath caught as her eyes met his. "You came back."

Tension hummed between them.

"I said I would." Light played in his eyes, defying the deep brown depths.

A tear dropped from her cheek. "I never gave up." She no longer cared what her father thought. She had almost lost him.

He shook his head. "I crossed miles and miles to hear you say that."

Silence cupped them in its hand, but Lena wouldn't know for the beat in her ears.

Victor held her face, tracing his thumb along her jaw. Her breathing hitched and gave way to sobs. Lena covered her mouth, not taking her gaze off him. "I can't believe it."

"Let me help you." He clasped her hands and swung her arms over his shoulders.

A laugh vibrated her lips, but he stilled her with a gentle brush of his mouth. He pulled back, examining his work as her cheeks bloomed pink. The crowd had thinned around them, but Havenville was a small town and even the streets would speak.

She inhaled and closed her eyes. Victor could be dead, and nobody would know about their love. Lena would shout it to the world. She stretched in his arms, finding his lips again. This time would be forever.

Their kiss deepened and her mouth opened to him, inviting him to claim that part of her life which she would give to no one else. He groaned against her in acceptance, sending her stomach into cartwheels.

"I never doubted your word," she lied.

He raised her chin. "I'll never give you a reason to again."

Experimenting with the Dance of Death

Cray Dimensional

Becca raised her hospital bed to look at the prom gown images displayed by the holoprojector. She didn't have any prom proposals yet, but she planned to ask her best friend Martin, an exchange student from the planet Kepler. She closed her eyes and imagined his translucent lips kissing hers but returned to reality when one of the monitors in the room beeped, reminding her she didn't have long to live. Should she even ask Martin? It wasn't fair to burden him with her and her bald head. Why couldn't she be an ordinary high school senior, shopping for a prom dress instead of being stuck here in Philadelphia's Saint Angus Hospital, hoping for a miracle?

Becca focused back on the prom. Anything was better than staring at the wardrobe or the egg-shaped chairs on either side, reminding her of her cancer. She put her noise-canceling earbuds on and scrolled through the images of prom gowns, stopping on the Golden Galaxy Dust one. It was perfect. It was self-fitting, and the sleeves would cover her IV marks. She wouldn't let a malignant tumor keep her from her dreams. The prom was only two weeks away, and here she was, looking at sterile white walls while breathing in the mint fumes of cleaners. She wanted to go and feel Martin's warm arms holding her as they danced to the song "A Kiss to Die For." It wouldn't happen. Dad was too obsessed with keeping her safe to let her go.

She was so engrossed in dress shopping, she didn't notice Martin walk in until she picked up the musky scent of his cologne. Her heart beat so fast that the guards, six stories down, could hear it. She liked how his veins, bones, and muscles showed through his translucent skin. His slicked-back blue hair completed the look. What was he hiding behind his back?

Becca smiled, pulling out her earbuds. "Martin? What are you doing here?" She wiped her sweaty hands on the blanket covering her. She had to ask now before clouds of self-doubt rolled in. "Will you go to the prom with me?"

Martin laughed.

Becca crossed her arms. "Why are you laughing? Am I a joke now?"

Martin's eyes gleamed with mischief. "You are certainly not a joke. Let me show you something." He got down on one knee and pulled out a red velvet pillow with the words: *will you go to prom with me* embroidered on it. "I came here to ask you, but you beat me to it."

Becca laughed, seeing the irony of the situation, but her happiness didn't last." Her mind twirled through questions. What if she didn't survive the tumor drilling into her brain? What if Dad wouldn't let her go? How could she dance when her body ached? Martin always seemed to know what she wanted, but he might not be able to deliver this time. She wiped her eyes.

Martin tucked the pillow under her head and sat in a chair beside the bed. "Hey, I didn't mean to upset you. You asked me first, remember? Don't you want to go?"

"I do, but what if I don't make it or my dad doesn't let me out?"

"Stop thinking like that. You'll make it. Your dad's the best doctor on the East Coast. He'll find a cure." He squeezed her hand. "And if not, I'll kidnap you for the night."

"Promise?" she said, holding out her pinky.

Martin wrapped his pinky around hers. "Pinky promise."

There was a knock at the door. "Baby girl, can I come in?" Great, it was Dad.

Becca grinned at Martin. "You'd better hide. Dad doesn't like me talking to boys, especially alien ones who plan on kidnapping me."

Martin laughed. "No problem, all I have to do is take your dad to Kepler. That way, I won't be the alien. He will be."

She slapped his hand. "You're incorrigible. Now serious, how about getting in the wardrobe?"

He winked. "I'm not going anywhere. Besides, I want to meet your dad."

Becca sighed. "Don't say I didn't warn you." She took a deep breath to calm down her nerves. "Come on in."

Dad entered, followed by her nurse bot, Janet, who wheeled her short rectangular form to the beeping monitor.

Dad adjusted his glasses and pulled out a tablet. "I think we're finally making progress," He looked around, fixing his eyes on Martin. "Who's this?"

"Dad, meet Martin. He's my b—my friend from school. Martin, this is my dad, Dr. Gregory Simon."

Dad's eyes rolled from Martin back to Becca. "Nice to meet you, Martin."

Becca wrung her hands. Now was as good a time as any to announce her plan. She wasn't going to give him the option of turning her down. "Martin is taking me to the prom."

Dad coughed. "Martin, would you mind leaving? Becca and I need to talk."

"Yes, sir, Dr. Simon," Martin said, standing up.

Becca grabbed his arm and pulled him toward her. "No. Stay," she said, staring down at Dad. "Whatever you have to tell me can be said to Martin."

Dad's face turned bright red for a second, then relaxed into a non-revealing doctor-patient expression. "The chemotherapy shrunk the meningioma, but there is a risk it will continue to metastasize. The only option aside from increasing the dosage is surgery. That means you will not be able to leave the hospital for another three weeks."

Becca swallowed to open her tightened throat. She refused to break down. "Stop talking to me like a doctor. I am your daughter. What do you mean another three weeks? I have already been in and out of the hospital for six months while you fiddled around with various treatments and surgeries, and now even chemotherapy won't work. That's it. I'm eighteen. Which means I am an adult. I don't give you permission to continue treatments. I'm going to the prom. You can experiment all you want after that."

"Becca honey, I wouldn't ask if I had another option. This is my last resort. This tumor doesn't match any known type of meningioma. I'm afraid of what will happen if we wait much longer. Please, this is our last chance. I don't want to lose you. Besides, you are not eighteen for a few more days."

Becca tried to pull herself up but winced and fell back onto the mattress. She wouldn't give up that easily. "Don't you think I know the risk? It's just that I missed so much already, and nothing seems to work. I can't miss the prom too. If I'm going to die, I want to have one happy high school memory before I go."

Martin turned to Dad. "Sir. Let me grant her this one wish. I'll take good care of her. I promise. I'll make sure we bring a hover chair in case she gets tired."

Dad's forehead wrinkled. "It's Martin, isn't it? Are you Keplerian? I heard they speak mind to mind. Is that true?"

"Sort of. I guess you can call it talking. But only with other Keplerian. Earthlings don't have the capacity."

Becca rolled her eyes. "Dad. Stop changing the topic. I don't need a lesson on Keplerian linguistics. I am going to the prom. The treatment can wait."

Dad lifted her chin. "Honey, look at me. You've been strong for too long. Just hang on for a little more. I have another idea." Dad glanced at Martin and then back to Becca. "Give me one more week. Let me prove to you that we can beat this tumor."

Becca pushed him away. It was always one more day, one more week. But she was tired of fighting. "I'll give you a week. No chemo. Then I go to the prom, regardless. Promise me."

"I'll do my best." He patted her head and then walked toward the door, beckoning Martin to follow. "Well, Martin, how about we let Becca have some much-needed rest," he said. "By the way, do you know you have an interesting brain? What's that second module clinging to the spinal cord do?" Their voices faded, leaving Becca alone with Janet, thinking about how Dad was careful not to promise. She could only go to the prom if she fought for it.

"Janet, can you do me a favor?"

"Sure, deary, what is it?"

"Can you watch Dad and tell me what he's doing?"

"Sorry, but us nurse bots are programmed to keep information between doctors and nurse bots confidential. All I can do is watch and learn."

Becca closed her eyes and put her hand to her forehead. "That will have to do then. Just learn."

"Do you need something for your headache? Maybe a painkiller or coffee?" Janet said.

"No. I'll be fine. I just need to rest a little." Becca lied. She wasn't fine, but she knew Janet had other patients that needed her.

"Alright, but feel free to call me if you need something," Janet said, rolling out of the room.

* * *

A few days later, Dad stopped by her hospital room with a small syringe full of blue liquid.

"What's that?" she said, resting on her new pillow.

"It's anesthesia. I am going to perform a minor operation to attach healthy tissue to the tumor to coax it to produce the right cells. It's an experimental treatment," Dad said.

"Will it hurt?"

"No, you'll be asleep. The procedure will be performed by a microbot that I control remotely. So, the incision will be the size of a needle-head."

"Can I still go to the prom?"

"Let's just see how it goes. You want to feel better, don't you?" Dad's face revealed nothing, but he usually stuck to proven methods.

Was she going to live long enough to go to the prom? Each day she lost more of her mobility. Thinking about Martin's calls was the only bright spot of her day, but none came. "Yes, but I'd like to go to the prom with Martin. Where is he? I haven't heard from him for days."

Dad looked down, avoiding eye contact. "Don't worry about him. Maybe he wasn't the right boy for you. There are plenty of other boys at your school. Let's just focus on getting you better first."

She wished she could punch the bed, but her arm ached. Wait. The last time she heard from Martin, he was with Dad. "Dad! You chased him away, didn't you?"

He shrugged. "Honey, you know I wouldn't do anything to hurt you."

"Then show me that."

"Tell you what, I'll find Martin after this treatment."

She shivered. Dad didn't understand. "I hate when you say that. Every treatment I've had makes me feel worse. Why can't you listen to me? I am your daughter, not your patient. I want to go to the prom with Martin. The treatment can wait."

Dad raised his voice. He'd never done that before. "No! It can't. You can barely sit up in bed now. Without this, you might not make it to any prom. Got that?"

She shrunk into her mattress, trying to get as far away from Dad as possible. What happened? He'd never been this anxious before. "I'm sorry, Dad. I didn't mean to upset you."

"No. I'm sorry. I didn't mean to yell. It's just that I don't want to lose you." Dad shook while he hugged her. "I know you're a fighter. Trust me. You need this, baby girl."

Becca's muscles tightened. She'd never seen Dad this shaken up before. Maybe she should have the procedure. It couldn't be worse than the others. Could it? Even if Martin had to carry her to the prom, she'd push through. That's if she could find Martin. She wasn't going to let Dad off the hook.

"Fine. I'll do it, but Martin better be here after I wake with a Golden Galaxy Dust gown in his arms. You bought it, didn't you?"

Dad forced a smile. "Yes. I picked it up yesterday," he said, pushing the gurney beside her bed. "Are you ready, baby girl?"

Becca looked down. "Wait. Do you mind if Janet watches? I don't want to be alone."

"Of course not," he said, pushing Janet's call button. "We'll wait for her."

It didn't take long for Janet to roll in. "You called? What do you need, Doctor Simon?"

Becca gave a weak smile. "I asked for you. Could you hold my hand during the surgery?"

Janet's yellow eyes changed to pink. "Certainly."

After Dad lifted Becca onto the gurney, Janet took Becca's hand.

"Alright. Once I add the anesthesia, I want you to count to 10. Got it?" Dad said, injecting the syringe into her IV line. One, two, three…"

Becca closed her eyes to make the room stop rocking.

* * *

Moments later, Becca was no longer on the gurney. Instead, she rocked as if on a boat being pushed around by waves. The familiar musky smell of Martin's cologne reminded her of her friend. "Martin? Is that you?" she said, opening her eyes, expecting to find him. Instead, she found herself in the mirror image of her hospital room, lying on a bed. The back of the door held a map with the number 6177 circled in red. She tried to lift her arm, but it didn't move. She looked down to see a translucent arm held down by a restraint. That couldn't be her arm. What was happening to her? She screamed, closing her eyes again.

She kicked her feet so hard that the bed shook. "Let me out of here!" She rolled against the bed rail.

Dad's voice broke through. "Baby girl, wake up. It's only a dream," he said, shaking her.

"Dad? Is that you?"

"Yes, open your eyes. You're safe."

Becca was back in her hospital room. She lifted her hand in front of her face, noting that it was as pale pink as before, but she couldn't see her veins and muscles through her skin. The traces of musk cologne morphed into pungent disinfectant cleaners. "What happened? I was in another room. I was a different person.

Dad smiled. "It wasn't real, just your imagination. Don't look now, but you are strong enough to lift your arm. That's progress."

Her arm didn't ache. "I can, can't I? How long have I been out?" She tried to get up, but the room spun around her. "Computer, raise the head of the bed," she said, hoping her dad didn't catch on that she wasn't feeling well.

"A few days. We kept you under for a little to allow some time for treatment to take."

She smiled. "Is the tumor gone?" she said, rubbing the back of her head to check for a lump. She felt the room fall out beneath her. Another disappointment. "I still feel a lump."

Dad put his arm around her shoulders. "Everything is going to be fine, baby girl. I ran a tumor biopsy, and it is realigning to the new DNA. Soon the malignant cells will be gone and all that will be left is a benign lump."

Becca scanned the room, eyes stopping on a golden gown hanging in the open wardrobe. Her heart did a flip. "Is that what I think it is? There's still time to go?"

"Yes. It's tomorrow. I'll drive you," Dad said, hands fidgeting in his lab coat pocket.

"You don't have to. Martin said he would take me."

"I'm sorry, honey, but Martin is on his way back to Kepler."

Becca looked away to keep Dad from noticing her disappointment. Martin wasn't just a boyfriend. He was her best friend. If she fell, Martin was there to pick her up. When she was sad, he'd tell jokes till she laughed. Every night they talked for hours on the holo-phone. He always knew what to say to cheer her up. But now he left without a text or a call?

I didn't! I'm here, a voice in her head said, though it faded away.

The voice felt like Martin, but she didn't see anyone. Her overactive imagination played a cruel trick.

Dad raised his eyebrows so high that his forehead wrinkled. "Honey, what's wrong? I thought you would be happy?"

"It's not the same without Martin. I'm tired. Leave me alone," she said, hugging her heart-shaped pillow.

Dad sighed. Then he leaned over her bed and kissed her forehead. "Sorry, baby girl. It'll get better. I promise. I'll be back in the morning." He left, closing the door.

Martin could have at least waited to see her before he left. He deserved better anyway.

* * *

Later that night, in her hospital room, Becca was woken up by a gentle nudge in her head.

Becca, Dew Drop, please wake up. It's important.

A musky cedar scent permeated the room. Funny, she didn't remember falling asleep or anyone entering the room. Even after her eyes adjusted to the darkness, she didn't see anyone. "Lights on." It had to be Martin, but no one was in the room but her. Once again, her imagination went wild.

You aren't imagining this. It's me, Martin!

"I don't see you," she said. How silly? She was talking to herself.

You can't see me because I am inside you. Or at least a piece of me is. Did you ever ask your dad where he got the tissue to graft onto your tumor?

"Sorry," she said, clapping her hand over her mouth. So that's why Dad was acting strange. "Why did you let him do that?"

I wanted to save you.

Becca swallowed. She wanted to live, but not like this. "What's going to happen to you?"

I don't know. I can't find my way back to my body.

Crying wasn't going to fix Martin. She closed her eyes and took several deep breaths, focusing on everything that happened after the procedure, including in her dreams. If Martin was in her head, then maybe, he left something there. Her memory wandered to the moment she had a translucent arm, Martin's. Her lips trembled thinking about him. It wasn't the time to lose it. To free him, she needed to look for clues in his room. She went through everything she remembered, stopping on the map with room number 6177. "Martin. Your body must be in room 6177. It's down the hall. I'm going. Guard rails down," she said, swinging her feet over the edge of the bed. Pinpricks of light flickered in front of her.

Hold on. You haven't been on your feet for a week.

She jumped onto the floor, refusing to listen. "Seeing stars is normal. I just sat up too quickly. Besides, if we make it to the prom, I want to dance—" Becca sniffled. "—with you."

But I am with you. Now. We can go to the prom, just like I promised.

"No. Not like this. I want to snuggle in the warmth of your arms. It's not fair to leave it like this."

Becca slid her compression stocking-covered feet into her slippers. She wobbled, grabbing her IV cart for support. She left the room.

See, you are in no shape to continue this. Use the computer to contact your father.

"No, I want to see for myself what he did to you."

She shuffled her feet down the white-tiled hallway, passing by Janet, the nurse bot, along the way.

Janet approached her. "Good to see you up and around, Becca. Shall I alert Dr. Simon?"

"There's no need to bother him. I was just looking for room 6177."

Janet's yellow eyes expanded from quarters to half dollars. "I'm sorry, but that room is off-limits."

Becca stood her ground. "Why?"

The bot moved in front of the black pocket door on the right. Judging by the musky smell, Martin's scent, this was his room. "Dr. Simon's orders. Are you hungry? I can bring your breakfast back to your room. Today's menu is a clear liquid diet."

It's a good suggestion. Dew Drop. You haven't eaten for a few days.

At the mention of food, Becca's stomach grumbled with hunger, instead of nausea. It was an opportunity to distract Janet. "Thank you. I'll get it back in my room." She shuffled back the way she came, not daring to turn around. She hid behind her door when she returned to her room, keeping it ajar long enough to see Janet leave Martin's room. Becca took a step outside the door but was interrupted by Martin.

Just know that I love… Martin's mind voice dissipated, leaving Becca alone to her thoughts. The quiet meant one thing. Martin was in trouble.

Becca sprinted out the door, her heart beating in double time. She wasn't sure where the extra energy came from, but she drank its nectar and ran to room 6177. From the corner of her eye, she saw Janet rolling toward her from farther down the hallway. Becca quickened her pace, arriving at the room. Janet was getting closer.

Becca opened the door but wasn't prepared for the sight before her. Martin shook in the bed, and Dad's pale, sweaty arms held him down. Judging by the extra gurney, the silver table with syringes, and a remote control, Dad must have just operated on Martin.

"Dad, what do you think you are doing?"

"I'm trying to save him."

"You're not. You're making him worse."

Dad rubbed his forehead. "I can't figure it out. I didn't take that much extra. The brain cells should have regenerated. Like they did before with you."

Becca shook her head. "I'm not hearing this. How much tissue did you take?"

Dad turned his face away from her. "Just enough to heal you. Plus, a little more to experiment with."

Becca put up her hand and backed away. She was going to lose her best friend, and it was her fault. Dad wouldn't have done this if she wasn't ill. "Dad, you have to put it back. He's dying."

"Don't you think I know that? The trouble is the experimental tissue died. The only living tissue left is inside you. I can't risk losing you too."

Martin's body stopped shaking, but the monitor showed a flat red line. Dad ripped off Martin's shirt and placed the defibrillator paddles on his chest. It took a couple of jolts to revive him.

Dad rubbed his forehead. "I don't understand."

Becca closed her eyes and took a deep breath. Only she could fix this. She walked over to Dad and put her hand on his back. "Dad, you know what you have to do. I am eighteen now, and I permit you to take the graft from me and give it back to Martin. The prom isn't important anymore. I can't live a stolen life, and I know you couldn't live with yourself, either. What's important now is Martin. Save him."

He hugged her. "I just can't. I can't say goodbye. I need you."

She wiped his eyes with a tissue. "Please. I promise, Dad. We'll find another way."

"No, I can't do it."

Janet rolled into the room. "Sorry, Doctor Simon. I tried to stop her."

Becca remembered Janet's words to her, learn. "Janet, you saw the operation. You learned it. Dad can't bring himself to do it. Please take a graft of my tumor, and give it back to Martin."

Dad sat in a chair and curled into a ball. "You must think I am a monster. Now that you're eighteen, you can make your own decisions. But I'm sorry. I can't do this for you." He turned to Janet. "Janet, I violated my oath. The doctor to nurse bot oath no longer applies. Take good care of my daughter."

Janet patted the gurney. "Hop in, deary."

Becca hopped onto the gurney and stretched her arm with the IV feed out. "Is this good?" she said, trying to keep her arm from shaking.

"Yes," Janet said, pushing the syringe into her IV line. "Don't worry, deary. This won't hurt a bit."

* * *

Within a few hours, the anesthesia pushed Becca into a slumber. She dreamed of a bright light at the end of a tunnel where Martin stood. She ran to him.

Martin took her hand. "Why didn't you accept my gift?"

She looked into his pink eyes. "My life for yours is not a fair trade."

"Who said it is an either-or situation?" he said, kissing her lips.

The light disappeared, taking Martin with it.

She sat on the tunnel floor, crossing her arms to protect herself from the chill. She never expected death to be so cold. Was she stuck here for eternity? She stared at the shadow of herself on the wall. Wait. If there was a shadow, then there had to be light. She turned around to see a spec of light no larger than the flame of a candle. She ran toward it, screaming. "I'm here," repeatedly.

* * *

Becca. Dew Drop. Wake up! Martin said.

But Martin left. Didn't he? She forced her eyes to open. Sure enough, Martin stood next to her bed, holding her hand. Her hospital room was just as she remembered, with her Golden Galaxy Dust dress hanging from the wardrobe.

"How am I alive?"

"You'll need to ask your dad about that."

Dad coughed. He sat on a chair next to the wardrobe, wearing just a flannel shirt and a pair of jeans.

"Dad, where's your white lab coat?"

Dad winced. "I broke my oath by going outside the parameters of the experiment with you and Martin. So, I will have to find a new job."

"But we're alive. Doesn't that count?"

"No. I was wrong. If not for you and Janet, Martin would have died. You saved him by volunteering to donate cells. Fortunately, by then, your cells learned to behave just like Martin's. Don't be surprised if there are side effects from this surgery though."

"Side effects? Like what?"

Martin grinned. *I can tell you how gorgeous you are without freaking out your dad.*

Becca's face warmed. "Can you hear me too?"

Yes.

Becca's eyes caught the prom gown hanging in the wardrobe. She had missed the prom, but she was alive. She refused the tear threatening to roll down her cheek. "I'm sorry, Dad, for making you buy the dress. You can sell it."

Dad coughed. "I will not. Why don't you put it on?" He winked at Martin.

I bet you look beautiful in it.

Dad and Martin left the room.

With the help of Janet, Becca put on the golden gown. She then covered her bald head with a matching scarf.

It's been twenty minutes. Can I come back in now? Martin's mind voice had a tinge of joviality to it.

"Yes," she said.

Upon entering the room, Martin smiled. "You are simply beautiful."

Her ankle twisted the wrong way, and she fell. Fortunately, Martin caught her. He carried her out the door into the hallway, stopping at the elevator.

"Where are we going?"

You'll see.

Once inside the bullet silver capsule of an elevator, he hit the lobby button.

"You know, you can put me down now," Becca said.

"Not yet," he said, squeezing her hand.

The door opened, revealing a dark glass-enclosed courtyard twinkling with faux star lights. High school teenagers danced to the song "A Kiss to Die For."

Becca looked into Martin's glowing eyes. "What'd you do?"

"I kept my promise to you. Even if I had to kidnap you, I promised I would take you to the prom." He placed her on the ground, and the two of them stared into each other's eyes.

The elevator door opened, letting out Janet. She rolled out toward them and pushed Becca into Martin's hands. "I think it's about time you two kissed," she said, darkening one of her yellow eyes in an attempt at a wink.

Becca laughed. "I think you're right," she said, pulling Martin's translucent lips to hers.

Just For This Moment

Keyra K. Allred

Amager, Copenhagen, Denmark. October 23, 1942.

Karoline entered the small flat amid a flurry of hushed chaos. Two men, one old, one just barely older than her own fifteen years, flew about the room, pointing and grabbing the few photographs tucked solemnly on shelves. A middle-aged woman walked hurriedly from the kitchen, shushing them all despite the surprising lack of sound.

"Wha...?" Karoline began and was immediately shushed by the trio, eyes widened in panic. The woman pointed toward a door at the back of the narrow hallway, all the while keeping her fingers to her lips, urging Karoline to stay quiet. Karoline nodded, confused, her terror growing with every second, especially when she caught sight of the sad expression on the woman's face.

What was happening? she thought.

Turning the knob, Karoline was met with a more subdued haste. Rachel moved about her bedroom, picking up items and staring at them for a melancholic moment before setting them back down exactly as they had been. Upon Karoline's entrance, Rachel spun, horror marring her beautiful features.

"Karoline," she breathed, some of the fear dispelling with the exhalation. Rachel dashed to the girl, enveloping her in a hug that threatened to take the life right out of her. Her friend's arms around her gave Karoline the peace lacking from the moment she had entered the flat.

Then she felt Rachel shaking against her. Great, heaving sobs wracked her entire body and Karoline found it difficult to hold the poor girl up. The violence of Rachel's emotions was too much and Karoline had to give up the fight, both of their bodies sinking to the worn wooden floor. Karoline's hand went to Rachel's head, stroking her hair, hoping desperately to calm her enough to know what on Earth was happening.

Rachel whined softly into her hair. Karoline tried to be patient but her threshold had been reached.

"I can't understand you. Please," Karoline begged. "What is happening? What's wrong?"

"We're… leaving," Rachel choked out, her words nearly lost to sorrow. Karoline's heart plummeted. Leaving?

"What do you mean that you're leaving? Where are you going?"

"I… don't… know!" Rachel moaned.

Karoline gapped, astonished. No, that couldn't be, she reasoned. Why would they leave without knowing where they were headed? "Why?"

"They're coming for us."

Karoline didn't have to ask who. She knew who. The Germans.

Threats had stopped being enough.

Now there would be blood.

Now she would lose her best friend.

Maybe forever.

"No."

"No?" Rachel asked, pulling away, confused.

"I won't lose you," Karoline said, resolved. It might be for a moment, this moment, but it would not be forever.

Rachel wiped at her snot covered face. "We're leaving tonight. I don't know if we'll ever be back. Yussef says not to count on it."

Karoline chuckled, holding the girl's face in her hands. "Like your brother knows anything?"

That, at least, got a smile out of Rachel.

"You are my best friend. We have been together nearly every moment of our fifteen years and we will be together again. We will find each other." Karoline stared into the deep ocher eyes that gazed back out at her with such trust.

Rachel nodded, slowly at first but then with a determination that belied her short years and tear stained face. "You are my heart."

Karoline shored up her courage, courage born of agony, boldness, and her time finally running out. She didn't have any more seconds to wait, to hope, to talk herself out of it. This was the moment. There wouldn't be another. Not for many years. But she didn't know that. She didn't know it would take them another fifteen years to find one another. To happen across each other outside of a cinema showing *An Affair to Remember* in New York City. For their eyes to meet, disbelief, happiness, heartbreak crashing together amid a crowd of oblivious passing people. She didn't know it would take fifteen years for their hearts to begin to heal, together.

Right now, she had this second and fear would not rule it. The rest of the world and all of its evils ceased to exist. This was for them. Giving Rachel a small smile, Karoline leaned forward slowly. She watched as Rachel's eyes widened in surprise, but her heart soared when the girl didn't pull away. Two pairs of lips met in a small bedroom in the soon to be abandoned flat of a six story building on an island in the middle of Scandinavia. It wasn't New Year's fireworks, it wasn't the booming of canons, it wasn't circling stars. But that didn't mean it wasn't magic.

It was tender. It was pure. It was perfect.

It lasted only seconds.

But love doesn't need eons. It can work with the here and now.

They pulled away, smiling softly at each other, their promise sealed.

A soft knock came at the door.

"Girls, I'm sorry. It's time for us to leave."

Exit 374

Angela Poole

She knew it was time for another pit stop. This time gas, snacks, and the bathroom. The sign on the side of the road told her Ontario was coming up.

Ontario, Exit 374. Never thought I'd be here again.

The new construction on both sides of the highway was unfamiliar to her but just thinking about coasting down the upcoming exit brought the memories flooding back.

If I take a left and follow the road through the bend, I would have to take the next right.

The light turned green and she took a right and pulled into the gas station. She drove around the building just like always making sure it looked clean and pulled into pump 8.

This was new. Of course, there are going to be a lot of new things twenty years later.

She slid her credit card and entered the zip code and started pumping the gas. She leaned against the side of her car.

It was twelve minutes. Twelve minutes from the exit to his house. I can't believe I remember that. I wonder if he stayed or where he went.

The pump clicked. She removed the hose and hung it up. The receipt spit out the slit and she pocketed it, made sure the car door was locked, and went inside. She headed to the back of the store where the bright blue arrow pointed to the Ladies room.

Twenty years makes you forget a lot, but not everything. The creaky steps on the covered porch, the butterflies, sitting in my car the first time I surprised him, wondering if I should go in.

She turned the water on and carefully leaned in to get soap.

My shaky hand knocking on the screen door. The door partially opened and me, peeking into the living room.

She pulled two towels and dried her hands, then grabbed two more and wiped off the counter.

Then there he was with that surprised look and then that smile. She felt a distance flutter in her stomach as she remembered his words. "Get in here girl."

She grabbed a Coke and then went to pick out a jerky stick. *Nothing too spicy. Perfect. Teriyaki.*

"Is that everything for you?" the cashier asked.

"Yes, thanks."

"Where ya from in Idaho?" a voice behind her said.

"Idaho Falls" she said as she turned. In an instant she fell back into the summer of 1987. *Mmmm, that smile.*

The Pull of the Stones

Erin Poche

Avery squinted at the monitor, using her laptop case to block the sun's glare. All around her, frantic travelers shuffled back and forth, lugging their bags. The train to Salisbury read, "Canceled-See Attendant." Groaning, she pulled her rain jacket flap over her head to protect against the constant drizzle and chill that hadn't ceased since she set foot on English soil.

She followed the crowd outside the station and approached a large plate glass window. Avery hoped she could understand the older man wearing a railroad conductor hat. Her clogged ears hadn't popped from the overseas flight from Boston. Since her painful earache on the plane, she only heard a muffled drone, like she had on thick, woolen earmuffs.

She had to be at Stonehenge by six p.m. or miss her private tour. "Excuse me," she showed the attendant her ticket.

He pointed to a long queue forming in the outside parking lot. "Take the bus to Andover; from there, you'll catch the train to Amesbury." He yelled through the glass.

"I have to take a bus to Hanover?" She strained to understand his accent.

He leaned forward as if she was dense. "Andover with an A," he snapped. The man drew a circle in the air for her to get moving.

She followed the masses to an outside parking lot where several buses lined up beside one another. "Great, just great."

Passengers grumbled, swearing profanities at the injustice and inconvenience. "Someone should get sacked for this, yea," said an angry man with his shoulders clenched to his ears. The crowd's agitation only increased Avery's anxiety. Either way, it forced her to "wing it," something entirely against her better nature.

She tried to calm her breathing—just one of life's little hiccups, her mother used to say. At twenty-five, she was already more jaded than her optimistic mom, who believed in horoscopes and fortune cookies. She gripped her shoulder bag across her chest. Nathan had warned her of pickpockets, a new band of hooligans who diverted your attention with small talk while they scanned your wallet for credit cards or cut your purse strap.

Avery put on her leather gloves and ski hat that read LONDON across the front. She didn't care if she looked like a tourist—there was no telling when the bus might arrive, and her damaged eardrums couldn't handle the cold.

A tall man with a scruffy beard and aviator sunglasses smirked at her hat. To make eye contact would only encourage him, the last thing she needed. It annoyed her; he didn't seem the slightest bit deterred by this setback, and he could lose the shades as there wasn't a bit of sun.

When she dropped the top of her water bottle, he lunged in a flash to retrieve it.

"Thank you," she said, feeling a little dizzy. She hoped her ear problems weren't causing her vertigo.

Someone with an oversized backpack knocked into her from behind, and she stumbled to right herself. The stranger caught her from falling off the curb. Avery drew a short breath at his touch and their proximity. She had to thank him again for his quick reflexes. They stood only inches apart now, and the forced intimacy felt jarring.

"This is so frustrating," she said, pulling her cap tighter over her blonde tresses. She tip-toed up and down for warmth.

He finally removed his pointless sunglasses to reveal twinkling hazel eyes. "Are you on holiday, then?"

"Yes, well, for work." She spoke louder than she intended with her clogged eardrums, probably sounding like a typical boisterous American. "I'm from Connecticut originally, but now I live in New York."

"Ah." He nodded as if that explained something about her. He grinned as if trying not to laugh.

The subtle arrogance in his ah rattled her. "What?"

"Nothing, nothing." His smile revealed a deep dimple in his left cheek and chin. "It's just your hat." He was much taller and thicker than her Nathan, but she decidedly preferred Nathan's height—they fit together perfectly, nose to nose.

"I had to buy the hat for my ears. I have a terrible earache from the plane."

He nodded, more concerned now. "That can be quite painful." The hovering crowd jostled them closer together.

"Very painful, yes. Are you from London?" She asked out of boredom.

"Nooo." He drew out the o. "London's full of criminals and shysters. I just met with both, actually."

His comment begged inquiry, but she refused to take the bait. Fortunately, the bus swerved through the parking lot, and the throng around her made a mad dash to form a line. Somehow, Avery got pushed to the rear. In her peripheral vision, she sensed the man watching her, not creepy, but protectively, in case she got knocked around again.

Avery reminded herself she was a taken woman. Though she wore no ring, Nathan, her boyfriend of five years, was officially her unofficial fiancée. He was even more pragmatic than Avery, and that was saying a lot. Nathan would finish grad school in August, and she had to write her dissertation this spring. They were busy grad students; the ring would come.

The thing was, she wasn't so sure lately. The wedding talk had chilled to the point where Avery felt awkward bringing it up. Nathan even began changing the subject whenever she discussed their buying a place together.

Lost in thought, she got squeezed to the back of the line and panicked when all the bus seats appeared to be taken. She frantically scrounged for an open spot, and the last available seat was next to the man who hated Londoners. He jumped to help with her suitcase, loading it into the overhead compartment.

"Thank you." Breathless, she plopped beside him as the engine revved and the bus took off. "I barely made it."

He smiled his cheeky grin, setting his hand before her. "Aidan Baglan."

She took his hand. "Where are you from? Your accent, are you—"

"Welsh."

"I thought maybe Irish." She brushed the touch of his handshake on her jeans.

"Yes, a Welshman can sound a bit like a Northern Belfast or Dublin accent, or Scottish even. And some might say there's a hint of Yorkshire in me, which is where my mother was from. My father's from Wrexham. It's in the north of Wales. That's where I grew up until I moved to Salisbury. I live there with my father now."

Great, a chatty Cathy, Avery thought.

"My mother passed away recently," he continued. "I've been meeting with her relatives in Chelsea."

"Oh, I'm sorry to hear that." Avery could empathize. She recently lost her grandmother, Kate, to lung cancer. The two were very close.

"Thank you." His piercing eyes appeared gray, almost blue now. Had they changed color?

She felt heat rising to her neck as their elbows touched. "I'm Avery Sloan."

"Nice to meet you, Avery Sloan."

His direct eye contact unnerved her. She pulled a book out of her bag, hoping tall, dark, and handsome might leave her to read. Though with the hum of the engine and warmth of the cabin, she found herself drifting to sleep.

After a twenty-minute cat snooze, Avery pulled out her notes for the Stonehenge tour. She covered her mouth to yawn, and suddenly, her ears popped back into working order. "My ears popped! I can hear." Her exuberance moved her to smile at Aidan with relief.

He slowly opened his eyes in amusement and stretched his arms overhead so widely that she thought he might put his arm around her for a moment. "You're going to Stonehenge, then?"

He was obviously reading over her shoulder. She closed her notebook abruptly.

"Sorry. I just saw your diagram. I work there."

"Really? I have a private tour there tonight."

"Are you an archeologist?" He asked.

"I hope to be an archivist."

"Avery, the archivist."

She liked hearing him say her name. "I'm working on my master's in medieval studies. The Solstice Festival is this weekend, right? Will it be very crowded?"

"Very crowded, you could say that. The town will be full of complete nutters dressed up in druid costumes." He rested his head back on the seat. "I dread this time of year. All the loonies come with their RVs and park along the freeway. We have to double the staff to keep them at bay."

It sounded like he worked security.

"I heard that the Northern Lights will be visible tonight."

"Aye. It's predicted tonight to be the strongest in the past few decades. You're in for a spectacular viewing, Avery." He grinned.

Her heart churned as she looked past him at the rolling countryside with its sprawling vistas. The scenery was breathtaking, with verdant hills and sporadic grazing sheep and cows. The Northern Lights excited her almost as much as the stones. They went through a tunnel, where everything went black.

The bus driver gave an update through a microphone, but Avery couldn't hear him over the quarreling elderly couple in front of them. "I can't hear HIM when you're talking to me!" The wife yelled.

"What did he say?" She asked Aidan.

Aidan laughed. "I couldn't hear." He pointed to the couple with raised eyebrows. "I think he said our stop is next."

"Honestly, I can't understand a word anyone says here, even if my ears weren't clogged."

"I might be offended; however, I understand your predicament. You get different accents from almost every town outside London."

"Everything's brilliant, lovely, or tosh." She leaned in to whisper, "What does tosh mean?"

"Tosh is complete rubbish. Someone's yanking your chain."

"I see."

"I'm sure you've heard 'lovely' a lot." He was flirting with those eyes again. Avery blushed, opening her book.

As they pulled into Andover, she saw a row of bright red, yellow, and brown brick houses situated on top of one another beside a cobbled bridge and a pristine flowing river.

Aidan helped with her bag, and she thanked him.

"I'll be seeing you then, Avery."

Doubt it, Avery thought as she boarded the next train to Salisbury, though she couldn't help searching for him among the passengers. Fortunately, this time, she could gaze out the window, which displayed a rich palette of forest green hills, a still creek and covered bridge, and more charming stone houses and crimson brick roads.

Once in Amesbury, a flock of peregrines took flight as she hailed a cab to take her directly to Wiltshire. The driver seemed to take the scenic route to Stonehenge. She barely made it in time for her six o'clock appointment.

Avery stashed her luggage under a covered patio and immediately searched for the stones. She had studied them for so long that it was thrilling to see them in the distance. Avery jogged to meet the other tourists mounting the shuttle. Panting, she stepped onto the bus and sat near the front. She prepped her camera and stopped to listen to a familiar Welsh voice.

It was Aidan from the train. She turned to see him walking with a clipboard, greeting people. He didn't look surprised to see her, "Hello, Avery." He seemed more business-like now as he addressed the group. His badge read, storyteller.

"Hello, I'm Aidan Baglan," he addressed the group. "I'm your guide today. I'm an archeologist and have studied the prehistoric monument for years. I live in the nearby town of Salisbury, and there's nowhere else I'd rather live. I have a few rules to go over before we begin the tour. First, please do not touch the stones. This is not a movie. You will not be transported back to 1760, Scotland. The stones have a fragile surface due to years of decay. It was built 5,000 years ago, and the circle was erected in the late Neolithic period about 2,500 BCE." He made eye contact with every traveler, even the children.

"It's actually a crime to touch them. I don't want to arrest you. I hate paperwork, so please don't touch the stones. And don't kiss the stones." People, including Avery, laughed. "They don't love you back. Don't brush up against them; if you do accidentally, please let me know."

How had she missed those dimples earlier today? Avery kicked herself for not picking his brain on the bus.

"And most importantly, don't get naked in front of the stones." The group chuckled. "Seriously, why do you think I have to say this? I wish I didn't have to. None of you were planning to get naked out there, hopefully?" He clearly had the crowd eating out of his hand.

It was only a two-minute ride to the monoliths. Avery's mouth opened slowly when the massive boulders came into view. Each majestic marker stood thirteen feet high and seven feet wide.

As they left the bus, she began snapping photos at once to capture the golden-haloed light piercing between two stones. The gloaming rays cast shadows that danced on the rocks, and the sunset prompted a mystical rose tint on the horseshoe ring of granite that caught in her chest. She almost walked through a wonderful spider web that clung between two stones, each weighing over twenty-five tons. Her heart hummed with excitement, taking notes and more pictures.

She heard Aidan speaking to some young children. "Ancient folklore says the wizard Merlin magically transported the stones from Ireland and had giants assemble them. King Arthur might be buried here himself. Or it could be a landing area for aliens." His eyes found hers.

"What do you believe about them?" She asked.

He beamed at her. "Well, Avery. As I'm sure you know, it was used as a burial site. Most of the buried bodies were facing the moon." Her pulse quickened as he turned her body toward the setting sun. "We can tell from the positioning there that it was also used as an astrological calendar, calculating solstices, equinoxes, and eclipses." He raised his eyebrows. "Others say it served as a ceremonial site or a destination for religious pilgrims. I think it was all of the above."

"Do you think the builders had the knowledge to predict such events, and how did they transport them?" A man from Melbourne asked, firmly planting his feet between them with his hands on his hips. He wore an Indiana Jones fedora.

Aidan shot her an apologetic nod. "Well, I agree with the Welsh geologist, Herbert Thomas, who said they dragged the bluestones from rafts along the Welsh coast and then up the River Avon. Thomas suggested that the people who carried the stones were Welsh and stayed here. My ancestors could be buried here."

An American family asked about the Northern Lights.

"If you can come back tonight, you won't regret it," Aidan told them.

The clouds met the horizon like puffy snow from a Botticelli painting. Then soon, a black, bruised fog blanched the sky, and the once beautiful day turned sour before their eyes. First, a drizzle and then heavy sheets that turned into tiny hail balls pounded the ground. Avery tightened her jacket straps as the tour group returned to the bus in the blistering rain. She wasn't about to be deterred. Avery paid for a full hour and intended to get it. Out of the corner of her eye, she saw only Aidan and the Melbourne tourist remain.

A faint curved rainbow of scarlet, yellow, and green shot across the rocks like a ghostly prism, so striking amidst the violent hail storm she paused to memorize it. Soon, the gorgeous sunny evening turned vicious with ominous thunder and lightning that zigzagged in the blue-patched sky, forcing them back to the bus.

Avery felt heartsick that the tour had ended so abruptly. She searched for the taxi driver's business card in her bag and punched in the number for the cab company, but no one answered. She called again, panicking, and it only rang and rang. Everyone exited the bus except for her. Aidan looked up at her with a slight grin. "Everything alright back there?"

"No. The cab driver isn't answering. I have no way of getting to my hotel." Outside, the rain pelted the glass from every direction.

"Are you sure you're dialing out correctly?"

"I am!" Avery yelled in frustration.

"Let me try." He called the number, then after several rings, called another company. "They're all closed. It's Sunday."

"That's ridiculous! I just took a cab earlier."

"Aye, but that was during the day. Give me a minute here, and I can drive you back to your hotel."

"Oh, thank you so much. I really appreciate it."

She should have felt awkward sitting in a stranger's car, but she seemed oddly at ease and still a little awed by the whole experience of the monument.

"Is that one of those safety whistles?"

She reddened at the rape whistle her mother bought her for the trip. "Sort of."

He grinned. "I bet your father bought it for you. A young girl, traveling alone to another country no less."

"My mother gave it to me. I never knew my father. He knew of me but didn't want anything to do with me. He had another family that took priority."

Aidan looked horrified by her intimate confession. "What a louse."

Avery laughed. "Yeah, you could say that. But my mom, grandmother and I were very close. They were all I needed. My Gram recently died, too."

"I'm so sorry." Her eyes misted.

As they pulled up to the Marriott, Avery offered him twenty pounds for the ride, but he refused. "Okay, well, thanks again!" She slammed the car door and met him at the trunk for her luggage.

"I know the bartender here. I think I'll have a pint while the rain dies down."

She nodded under her rain hood and let him pull her bag up to the lobby, where she got in line.

"Good luck to you, Avery." Aidan tipped his cap.

"Goodbye, Aidan." She smiled, wishing she could return to the Northern Lights, but all she wanted to do was shower and head to bed.

When she got to the front, the young clerk looked worried as he searched for her name. "I'm sorry, we've no rooms left."

"What?" Her chest squeezed. "I made a reservation!"

"I'm terribly sorry for the mishap. We've overbooked with the solstice."

"This is unacceptable. I've traveled all day. I want to speak to your manager."

The boy froze. "He's not here."

Avery snorted in disgust. "Well, can you suggest another place in town?"

"Everything's booked solid, I'm afraid." He moved to answer the ringing phone.

Avery's jaw dropped. Her toes and legs throbbed from the cold. Tears stung her eyes as she swallowed the lump at the back of her throat. Her head and left ear began aching. Her only hope now was that Aidan might have a suggestion. He knew the town and maybe had an inside connection.

She walked up to him seated at the bar, sipping his pint, talking away to the bearded bartender. The barkeep looked up to Avery. "Would you like a drink, miss?"

As Aidan turned around slowly, his face lit up to see her. A sudden warmth and familiarity emulated from this stranger—a kinship more than their simple acquaintance earlier. She had heard his laugh hundreds of times and knew how it felt to have his long arms draped around her. Avery didn't believe in déjà vu, but her brain told her otherwise.

"Did you get your room?" Aidan asked.

Her desperate situation snapped her back to reality. "No. No, they're out of rooms!"

Seeing a worried expression pass from him to the bartender, she wanted to collapse.

"Do you have any idea where I could find a hotel?" Her voice cracked.

Aidan pursed his lips. "Everything's booked in town because of the Northern Lights. During the solstice, both Amesbury and Salisbury are booked out for weeks."

Her eyes clouded, and she didn't trust her voice. "What am I going to do?"

The bartender began clearing the counter, eager to escape her breakdown.

Aidan pulled back the stool next to him. "Come sit. I might know of a place, but you won't like it."

Avery hesitated. "At this point, I have no options."

"You could stay with me and my pa. It's a small bed and breakfast run by our friend Kaleigh."

"I'll take it." She signaled for a beer and plopped down beside him. "Let me buy you dinner."

They moved to a private table and proceeded to drink more pints, and each had a beef pie.

"The planning and the effort it took to get the stones here." Avery felt flush and happy now to have a place to stay. "Pictures and videos don't do it justice. I had to stand here and see them for myself. So magnificent. I wish I could go back, but I'm going to Bath tomorrow to see the Roman baths." She shot him a kinder smile.

They talked for over two hours about their mutual love for museums, medieval history, and different cultures. "I want to know how the British Museum acquired the Parthenon Sculptures?" She asked.

"Well, they were quite naughty back in the day," Aidan said. "The Parthenon Marbles, Hoa Hakananai'a, the Rosetta Stone—all stolen, spoils of war."

Just then, the waiter brought their bill, and she snatched it before he could argue.

Feeling a little tipsy, she repeated herself on the way to his car. "Thank you for today. I wish the weather were better, but still, it was amazing." As he opened the car door, she thought once more what it would be like to have his arms around her. She decided she liked the faint scrub of hair covering his cheeks and chin, unlike Nathan's clean-shaven look.

Nathan. Tiny tics of remorse crossed her mind. Her phone died before she could return his texts from earlier. Avery had to pinch herself to remember Nathan once or twice during their meal when Aidan's glances lingered uncomfortably long. She had invited Nathan to come with her, but he declined, so she pushed her guilt aside.

They drove down a quaint cobbled road to a tiny brick house with a patch of wildflowers, two vibrant rose bushes and a willow tree in the front yard. Outside, crickets chirped in the cold night air, and an owl hooted.

"The sign blew down a few years back, and we've yet to replace it." Aidan sighed, opening the front door. "My father's not well. He's in a wheelchair now, so our guests are few and far between. They mostly hear about us by word of mouth."

The missing sign caused Avery to stiffen slightly, but the entryway had a front desk with several mail cubbies and key hooks, clearly indicating a bed and breakfast. She could hear Nathan's voice in her head chastising her for getting into a car with a stranger and going home with him.

She glanced at Aidan's profile and relaxed a bit. The feeling of that strange intimacy hadn't returned, but she trusted him.

"Kaleigh should have breakfast there in the morning." He pointed down a long hallway to a dining room with several small tables. She followed him up the split staircase, where he nodded to the bathroom. "Showers in there. Give the hot water a few minutes to warm."

"Thank you, Aidan."

After showering, Avery slipped into bed and fell fast asleep. A few hours later, she awoke to a gentle but firm pounding on the door. She pulled the covers up to her chin and lay stunned, afraid to move.

"Avery…" It was Aidan.

Slight anger overtook her as she wondered what kind of game he was playing. She threw on her Boston College sweatshirt and jumped out of bed. "What is it?"

"Get dressed and meet me downstairs."

"For what?"

"It's something you won't want to miss."

She closed the door and stumbled around the dark for her rain boots, not before stubbing her toe on the iron bedpost. She put on her London hat and grabbed her rain jacket, which was barely dry from earlier.

Car keys in hand, Aidan moved to the door.

"Should I have brought my bag?" Still half asleep, Avery wondered if a room had opened somewhere else.

"No, no." He shook his head, and she followed.

In the car, his heater rattled alive. They drove silently, and somehow, she knew he was taking her back to the stones. They passed several RVs, vans, and trailers parked on the side of the long road. Travelers sat outside their cars with tables of food and beverages. At the same time, musicians played strange Celtic music with drums that gave Avery the chills, or rather an electrifying nostalgia, as she looked toward the hills. Aidan drove up to the security guard at Stonehenge's entrance. "Rodney," he nodded. "Have you been up there?"

"Oh, it's quite a sight. You won't be disappointed."

Aidan drove as far as the road allowed. "The stones are closed off tonight." Along the way, Avery saw in the distant night a supernatural array of vibrant purple and orange hues catapulting across the Wiltshire night. Beyond the famous rocks, regal violet, sapphire and striking magenta shades lit the night sky. Battered, black clouds hovered with a scatter of brilliant, blazing stars glittering in the moonlight.

They got out of the car quickly without saying a word. Avery's skin felt hot and tingly, like when she last had the flu. She stared to the left and right, each vision more dazzling.

"Here's your Northern Lights for you."

She turned to face him, and they both smiled at the incredulous moment. People, friends of the museum with connections, had gathered around them. Most had cameras on tripods.

"Have you seen this—"

"I've never seen this before. It's a once in a lifetime—" Aidan looked at her now strangely, like he was seeing her for the first time. Their faces were inches apart. Aidan tilted his head and moved closer. His arms reached around and pulled her to him, as she imagined. His lips found hers, and the entire world dissolved around her. He took her face in his hands, and they slowly parted.

"I'm engaged." She regretted the words as soon as they left her.

He hopped up on the hood of his car and put his hands behind his head. "I don't see a ring."

She laid back beside him, and they stared at the glorious sky. After what felt like an hour, Aidan finally spoke up. "I have another surprise for you tomorrow before you're off to Bath."

"What is it?"

"Well, it wouldn't be a surprise if I told you now, would it?"

She grinned lamentably. "I bought my ticket; I have to be at the train station by one."

"We'll make time."

* * *

The next morning, Avery met Kaleigh, the cook and inn manager, a stout woman with a double chin and deep dimples. "I'm told to prepare a true English breakfast for you."

"That would be lovely." Avery sat reading through emails and texts on her phone. She finally replied to Nathan, and they planned a phone call later that evening. A few minutes later, Kaleigh delivered a plate of sausage, fried eggs, baked beans, cooked tomatoes and mushrooms.

"Thank you." Famished, Avery finished every bite. She then paid her bill with Kaleigh for the meal and room. Still, there was no sight of Aidan. It was nearly ten, and she thought about wandering around town alone. Suddenly, he burst through the door and asked if she was ready.

Avery shrugged and grabbed her rain jacket and purse. "Sure, not sure what for, but let's go."

She headed for the car, but he said, "We can walk there."

The deep green grass seemed lush and surreal from the day's previous rain. In daylight, the sandstone house and peach trees looked like something out of a fairytale. Finally, sunshine pierced through the clouds, and Avery felt a light, airy longing. She wished she could stay one more night but had a busy agenda to keep. It would be crazy to stay.

They strolled through the quaint town of Salisbury and crossed a bridge that led down Main Street, lined with coffee shops, pubs, and touristy gift stores.

"If you're a true archivist, you can't leave Salisbury without seeing this."

She had heard of the famous Salisbury Cathedral but had tours scheduled for Westminster Abbey and St. Paul's before she left London.

"Eight hundred years of history here. It's Britain's tallest spire at four hundred and four feet. Did you know it has the Magna Carta and the oldest working clock in Europe, dating back to the late 1300s? Now, how could you leave without a peek?"

Avery's smile deepened as she stared at the dreamy Gothic shrines and stone tombs. If the outside of the cathedral was stunning, the splendor of the Cloisters and Morning Chapel inside left her breathless. "What was I thinking, not coming here?" She snapped photos and read over the ancient charter to limit King John's tyranny.

"Come on. You're not afraid of heights, are you?" Aidan asked.

Avery thought back to getting woozy at the top of the Statue of Liberty but refused to let anything dampen this experience. "No."

They climbed fifty steps to a grand overlook of the main hall and chapel. Behind her, the detail of the stained-glass etchings from the 13th century took her breath away.

"Keep moving." Aidan opened another door and closed it behind her. "We have a tight schedule."

She suddenly realized they were the only ones in the cathedral. "How did you get us in here?"

"I have friends in high places."

They climbed another one hundred steps up a circular stone stairwell. The granite had grooved foot patterns worn down from years of use. Then, they ascended more spiraling stairs. However, these were wooden. They stood high above an overlook with countless wooden arches and elongated supported pillars. "These diagonal beams were added in the 16th century."

Next, they entered the stately clock chamber, and Avery followed him up another wooden staircase to the bell chamber. She stopped to admire it briefly before Aidan tugged her sleeve. "You feel alright? Not lightheaded?"

She nodded, and Aidan led her to another circular stone staircase, the smallest. Avery thought it would have been unsettling if one were the claustrophobic type.

Aidan pulled a tiny door open that revealed a tight balcony. Avery gasped at the view.

They stood still, and she pressed her hands on the cold iron railing. White, billowy clouds hung low against patches of pristine powder blue sky; a falcon drifted high before them. Everything froze below; the town stretched for miles in both directions. Shadows cast stark, dark lines across the emerald hills and the cobalt river Avon alongside the cathedral. A flock of tiny geese settled on the river bank.

The sprawling village, surrounded by mountains, flooded her senses. Her heart drummed in her chest. *I'm at home here*, she thought, feeling the same familiarity with Aidan, a longing she couldn't place, though stronger than before—like she belonged here.

"The cathedral caught fire in the late 1300s, and the townspeople had to bring water from the river in buckets." He pointed below. "They formed a chain that lined up from here to there and didn't stop until the fire was out."

A light crinkle of rain dusted their hair and shoulders. She drew in a small breath in amazement. A charge struck when his cold fingers touched her neck and ran down the base of her spine. Aiden caressed the back of her neck and kissed her softly. She held her eyes shut until they parted. She swallowed and cleared her throat. He backed away, a little surprised. Then he took her hand up to his lips and kissed it, rubbing her fingers in his. "Tell me, what kind of a fella asks a girl to marry him without a ring?"

An odd sensation gnawed at her chest like her heart itched, and she couldn't scratch it.

She ignored his question and pointed to the fantastic scenery. "Aidan, this is incredible."

He smiled back, clearly pleased with himself. "I thought you might like it. If you weren't afraid of heights."

"Oh, I'm afraid." She laughed. "But this, this was worth it." Her fingers inched across the railing, afraid to move too close to the edge. She had known this man for less than twenty-four hours but somehow felt utterly safe with him. Much sooner than it took with Nathan.

"Well, I should get you back then."

She took his hand. "Aidan, wait. Thank you for taking me here. I thought last night was amazing, but this, this view." She imagined the village as it was long ago, widening and growing larger with time. "This place, there are no words."

"I agree." He stared at her, unsmiling now. "Ladies first."

After retrieving her bags, they drove to the train station in silence. The entire drive, Avery focused on Nathan and why she needed to get back to him. They lived together and loved one another; they were engaged to be married, or were they? Looking at Aidan, she touched her lips where he kissed her only moments earlier. Her future plans with Nathan seemed fractured somehow.

Her slight irritation toward Aidan returned, his smirking at the train station. He should have told her he was the tour guide. He was disrupting her perfectly planned life now. Then she thought of their conversation at dinner and their shared love of history and the mystery of it all, something Nathan could never relate to. If she had more time here—

Avery pulled out her ticket for the turnstile. Aidan grabbed her suitcase from the back seat and walked with her to the platform.

His face grew grave, and he turned to her and blocked her path. "Stay."

Avery paused, searching his eyes. She didn't know him. He was a complete stranger, who wasn't a stranger, really. "I—

There was a new charge between them today. Their alchemy shifted, and all at once, she knew what she had to do. She wasn't worried about her thesis, Bath, missing the train, or, least of all, Nathan.

Before she could change her mind, Avery threw her arms around him, and they kissed for the third and then a fourth time. The train came and left, though everything felt right with the world, and nothing mattered as long as he was beside her.

"I've waited my whole life for you," He murmured in her ear.

"What did you say?"

"Stay." He kissed her again.

Avery let her ticket drop to the platform. She wasn't sure why she didn't get on the train or why she stayed in Salisbury. She only knew that she wanted to explore the why.

Winning Back Molly

Jonathan Reddoch

Francisco would do anything to win back Molly. Those eyes, that hair, those perfectly manicured nails. And teeth so white they sparkled like diamonds. She was his heart's truest desire. But she was unobtainable.

He missed cuddling her on the couch, waking up with her breath on his neck. The way she would never let him pee alone.

They had been constant companions since her birth.

She was of course the thoroughbred champion basset hound that now legally belonged to his wicked ex-wife Alita. She paraded Molly around town in a little baby buggy, taunting him, as all the people *oohed* and *aahed* at Molly's cute little bonnet. Those puppy dog eyes could not be ignored.

Francisco called his lawyer. He demanded they litigate. "Call the mediator! We have to get custody of my precious baby girl! Take this to the Supreme Court if we have to!"

The law offices of Dewey, Dewey, and Dulcet would gladly charge him an arm and a leg to take this matter back to court, but his attorney sat his client down and gave him the straight talk.

"We spoke with your ex-wife's counsel. At this point, it is highly unlikely that your ex-wife will voluntarily concede the animal's custody. So pursuing mediation is unlikely to yield satisfactory results. And frankly, I think the odds of a judge re-opening a settled divorce hearing for this is extremely unlikely. I'm sorry."

"But Alita has to have a price. I'll pay anything."

The lawyer thought a moment, "Just between you and me, her price is your suffering. She doesn't really care about the dog. She just doesn't want you to have it."

Francisco thanked his lawyer for his time, and wandered off to think.

Technically Molly was a wedding gift from her parents, so the canine was "hers" on paper, but Molly only ever bonded with Francisco. Alita never wanted to take care of Molly. She hated the walks and all the responsibility. Despite being exceedingly greedy and selfish, she was even more spiteful.

His lawyer offered some parting wisdom, "There are always more dogs in the sea—or kennel. My advice is to move on and find a new pet to love."

* * *

Fransisco paced the aisle, examining each prospect.

Bonbon was energetic, maybe too energetic.

Calypso chased its tail frantically like a maniac.

Gonzo wouldn't stop yelping at the wall.

Lilac was pretty but just not his type.

Rorgie was an adorable little mutt with a great demeanor. He could see Rorgie and him frolicking in the park, tossing the ball, Molly's favorite red ball.

He patted Rorgie's mixed coat gleefully. They could be happy together.

No! It wouldn't be right.

He just wasn't ready to move on. To love again so soon.

Maybe one day he would return and adopt them all. But not today.

"What a handsome fella," a woman cooed.

"Who me?" said Francisco, forgetting himself.

The woman laughed. "Are you adopting this little cutie?"

"He's a friendly gentleman. I was considering it." They both reached down to pet Rorgie, accidentally touching hands. "—But I just had my heart broken. By the devil."

"A devil dog?" she mused, claiming the dog into her loving arms.

"No, Molly was an angel, held captive by Satan herself."

She held out Rorgie to lick his face, "Any way we can help?"

"Well… there might be a way."

She smiled. "I'm Sally by the way."

* * *

Alita motioned for Sally to join her on the velvet couch (the one too fancy for dogs). "Please, sit."

"Thank you for taking the time to meet with me."

"Of course. Happy to meet another collector."

Sally hid her bemused expression behind a false smile. "She has a gorgeous coat. And those eyes! And that sad little droopy face. What is her name?"

"I named her Monique." Alita shrugged. "But she only answers to Molly."

Molly perked up at the sound of her real name.

"Ahh Monique is a beautiful name. For a beautiful dog."

"Yeah, she's OK."

"I would love to make an offer."

"Well, she's not really for sale. I can't part with Molly." She smirked. "For sentimental reasons."

"I understand. I want to pair her with my own male."

Alita's ear perked up. "If it's breeding you're after, I could loan her out. For a price."

"Let's arrange for a breeding plan."

* * *

"Hello?" Alita answered. "How is the breeding coming along? Are they getting along?" Alita enjoyed the break from dog duty but was anxious to have her precious emotional hostage returned.

"I'm so sorry to inform you," Sally said, "Moll—I mean Monique ran out into traffic and was hit by a truck."

"How could you let this happen?"

"I am so sorry. I will compensate you of course. Double what her market value is."

"Double!? Make it triple!"

"OK, of course, triple. I know how rough it can be losing a beloved pet."

"Yeah, sure, fine. Venmo me. Excuse me, I have to deliver the bad news to my ex." She smiled to herself with horrible glee.

Alita showed up in person unannounced to deliver the news to Francisco.

"Well, sorry Frannie boy, but your precious little doggie is dead. The little dummy got hit by a truck chasing a ball like an idiot." She could hardly contain her psychotic relief.

Francisco nodded. "Thank you for telling me. The poor little dear."

"Yeah, I know how much you loved it. More than your own wife..."

"Is now the time for petty grievances?"

"OK, I'll save them for next time." She gave an uncomfortable chuckle. "But it's just a dog."

"Not to me."

"So long, Fran..." Seeing his countenance fall, she actually shed a tear. She had finally gone too far.

She gave him a hug and walked off, for the last time, never to return.

"OK, she's gone!" he shouted.

Molly ran out from the backyard and licked his face. Oh, how he missed those kisses.

Sally came out after, trailed by Rorgie.

"I owe you one," he promised.

"You owe me a lot!" she said, wagging her finger.

"Well, how about we start with dinner?"

She kissed his cheek. "I think you owe me a lot of dinners, handsome fella!"

Ilona's Statue

Doug Gibson

Ghosts don't move on the wings of the wind. They trudge slowly, methodically to a purpose. The specter, named Istvan, began his journey in Siberia, where he died. Three months later, he passed Lake Deseda, on the outskirts of Kaposvar, Hungary. The city's cemetery drew closer.

At the Cimetiere Keleti, the Russian soldier, Major Rublev, approached the grave of Ilona, a 16-year-old girl he had lusted after. He was only there to see the white statue built for her, which read, "The beautiful teen died just before her wedding. Ilona remains our 'Bright One.'"

Major Rublev sneered. He felt no love or regret. Just fury that this young whore had denied him further pleasures. When he came to this city, Ilona's youth and beauty had painfully aroused him. He approached her. She spurned him. That was a big mistake.

She had a boyfriend, Istvan, a weak boy laughingly preparing for a career as a university professor. Major Rublev accused Istvan of treason. The Major's lies were the law. Istvan was taken far away from Hungary, and disappeared.

Ilona came to his quarters once. She begged him to save her love. Oh, how sweet it was to see her chastened. Major Rublev forced himself upon her. Her parents were threatened. He set a wedding date, with an aimless promise of mercy for Istvan. Of course, the Major made no effort to save Ilona's lover. Istvan would die in a labor camp.

Everything was far colder in the cemetery. Major Rublev moved closer to the statue. In smaller text, the inscription read that she had died of meningitis washing her hair three days prior to their wedding. How silly.

The night Ilona washed her hair, it was -10 Celsius, with strong winds. Ilona drenched her hair outside until she collapsed.

Major Rublev heard hissing as the night deepened to impossible cold. He achingly turned around. *The statue is alive* was his last rational thought. Those near the cemetery heard terrifying screams. The Major's body was discovered the next morning with a sharp branch thrust through his chest. His eyes retained the horror of his final moments.

The ghostly figure of the teen girl moved through dense trees and tightly packed tombstones. She wound her way tiptoeing between gravesites. Out of the grave, with senses only the dead enjoy, Ilona was aware of other spirits.

There was Istvan's mother, a woman dead ten years now. "He is coming, a kedvesem, my loved one."

Ilona was at the far end of the cemetery. Another specter emerged from the late-evening fog. The lovers Istvan and Ilona embraced. Hands clasped, they committed to an eternal love.

Now, many years later, legend has it in Kaposvar that late at night one can catch a faint glimpse of the two specters walking together, clearly in love. One sees Istvan's and Ilona's legendary love… and hears the groans from within the defeated, weathered, abandoned grave of the forgotten Major Rublev.

Despite All the Years

Debra Birdwell Winkler

When he came up to my register, I knew he looked familiar. Dressed sharply in a green polo shirt and tan trousers,
he was clean shaven with short brown hair graying at his
temples, intelligent-looking brown eyes with gentle crow's
feet showing. Just shy of six feet, I surmised. Attractive
with a nice face, but he looked a bit agitated with a deep
furrow in his forehead, no smile. Oh well, he was probably
a customer I'd helped before.

Then, it hit me. Despite all the years, I recognized the
handsome man before me. But would he recognize me? My
heart skipped a beat.

"Hello, sir," I began cheerfully, hoping for some kind of
spontaneous recollection on his part, "Is this everything you
need today?" I picked up the set of red silky pajamas, searching for the price tag. "You know, sir, we have a buy-one-get-
the-second-for-half-price-sale on these pajamas today."

"No, this is all." His deep baritone voice was firm,
almost harsh.

He wasn't even looking at me. I was hurt and just a little disappointed.

"So, large is the correct size, sir?" I paused, waiting for an answer.

"This is fine." He whipped out his wallet. "How much?" He didn't notice me. I was just a salesclerk unworthy of his attention.

You don't recognize me? Well, I can play your game.

I rang the purchase. "$42.46, including tax."

"That's an awful lot for one pair of PJs," he snapped, no eye contact at all.

"It's our finest quality, sir." I glanced at his open wallet. "If you buy two and use your card, it would only be $10.00 more." I smiled my grandest smile.

"I'm paying with cash." He slammed down a fifty-dollar bill, quickly flipping his wallet closed.

"That's terrific, sir."

After handing him the change, I carefully wrapped the pajamas with tissue paper, arranged them in a logo bag, then adjusted another tissue sheet in a nice array.

"Thanks for shopping with us today, sir."

"I don't need any frills, madam." Taking the bag, he pulled out the tissue paper and threw it on the counter. He looked right through me. "Can't you just give me this in a simple brown bag?"

The check-out line was getting longer. The other cashier had taken her break and I was the only open line.

"Would you please hurry, mister?" an impatient woman cried out from behind him.

"One moment, ma'am," I remarked sweetly to her. "I'll be right with you."

"Well?" He was irritated.

"Our logo bags are the only ones available for merchandise." I looked up at him. Waiting. Hoping. Nothing.

Finally, reaching under the counter where my purse was stashed, I unloaded my earlier grocery store purchases from a brown paper bag. "I have this bag, sir. Will it do?"

"Fine. But please hurry. I have someplace to be." He still had a bit of a Southern drawl.

Oh yes, I remembered him, but he obviously didn't remember me!

I placed his purchase into the brown bag. Before I could hand it to him, he grabbed the bag from the counter and marched out the store, pushing through two shoppers.

"What was his problem?" the impatient woman grumbled.

It took me a second to respond to her. I was hurt that he didn't remember me. I took a deep breath. *Oh well.*

Without answering her question, I just smiled and said, "Wow, I see you've picked out this pretty pink robe. It's my favorite." Smiling, I added, "By the way, if you add the matching gown with this robe and use our store credit card, you'll get ten percent off the set?"

The workday eventually ended smoothly, and I headed toward the door with my grocery purchases in a logo bag.

By the end of the day my manager, Imogene, was vexed beyond her breaking point. Today, we did very well with the summer sales traffic. That didn't matter. I knew she'd harp on something she said I did wrong. She always did.

"Well, Misty, you did okay today."

"Thank you, Imogene."

The store's policy was for a manager to inspect all objects carried out by employees at the end of shifts. She gave my purse and bag a thorough inspection, touching and turning each item in both to guarantee I'd not taken something without paying.

"What was with that horrible guy at the register earlier this afternoon?" She held onto my things as she spoke.

I shrugged. "He was in a hurry to be somewhere."

"So, because you gave him your grocery bag, you now have your groceries in our logo bag?" Her voice had a tinge of sarcasm. "You know each of these bags cost the company a dime a piece and you're just wasting this one."

I was always sweeter than sweet with Imogene. She didn't like me. I was twenty years her senior and, in her estimation, getting too old to work in this boutique. That's what other employees had told me. I certainly wasn't going to give her the satisfaction of turning me out to pasture. I was her best salesperson, even though she'd never admit it.

"Just trying to please our customer, Imogene."

"Well, stop being so friendly with the customers," she nagged, her face contorted as she reprimanded me.

She pushed my bags at me and then came the attack. "Because you took your time chatting with him, your line was too long, and several disgruntled customers complained to me about your slowness. Tomorrow, keep conversations at two to three minutes, understand?"

"Yes, ma'am."

***

At noon the next day, the guy was back. When I saw him, I cringed and thanked my lucky stars I was occupied with another customer. Each time he was next in line with the other cashier, he waved the person behind him forward.

When I was free, I called to him, "Sir, how may I help you today?"

"Remember me from yesterday?" he asked. He seemed in a much better mood today, although still no hint he recognized me.

I smiled. "Of course, sir."

He positioned the familiar brown bag on the counter between us. "These PJs won't do."

I opened the bag and pulled out the pajamas, still wrapped in tissue paper. "Was it the pajamas themselves, sir? Were they the wrong size? Or was it something else entirely?"

When he didn't answer immediately, I glanced up.

"Your name is Misty?" he asked.

My heart was in my throat as I lifted my name lanyard. I tried to be casual. "Yes, sir. That's what it says on my name tag."

"I've only known one person named Misty in my entire life."

So, maybe you do remember?

I could feel Imogene nearby so needed to be total business right now.

"Well, it's not a very common name anymore." I loosened the red pajamas from the tissue and didn't look at him. "Did you want to exchange it for something else?"

When I finally looked up, he was just staring at me. "Is there something wrong with the pajamas, sir?" I gave him my most radiant smile.

"Ah… well," he began, "they're… ah… they're the wrong size and color." He stopped.

I focused on the pajamas. "What is the correct size, sir?"

"Well," he stammered. "She… ah… needs extra-small."

"No problem, sir, we can find that for you," I responded, smiling again.

"Great!"

Trying not to let my hands shake, I asked. "And what color does your wife want?"

"Black." He smiled. "She wants black."

"Fine, sir. Let me find someone…"

Imogene interrupted, "I can help you, sir."

"No," he said decisively, as he turned my way. "I'd like Misty to help me with that, please."

I frowned, for Imogene's benefit.

Is that a twinkle in your eye I see?

"She'll be on the register for a while, sir."

I carefully refolded the pajamas, placing them back in the bag.

His voice was casual, not angry. "Then, I'll wait." He looked at her lanyard. "Oh, you're the store manager on duty."

"Yes."

"This salesgirl was a great help yesterday, so I want her to help me today. if that's okay with you."

I handed him the bag.

With a big smile, he said, "Thank you, Misty. I'll just wait over here until you're available."

"There's a chair right next to the entrance door," Imogene stated flatly.

"I'll wait." He slowly made his way to the chair Imogene indicated and sat like a king on a throne.

Imogene gave him a plastic smile and said to me, "Continue, Misty."

"How may I help you, miss?" I asked the next customer.

About fifteen minutes later, Imogene told me to check out.

In the office, I counted out my drawer in front of Imogene, who signed off on the register paperwork.

"Now, go help that rude customer."

"I don't think he was exactly…"

"Don't contradict me, Misty. Just get him out of the store," she ranted. "He's just a nuisance. I can help him as well as you can!"

I smiled and rushed out of the back office. Entering the main store, I bumped right into him.

"Sorry," I said as sweetly as possible, hoping upon hope he'd say something about remembering me. But nothing.

All he said was, "Find me the pajamas I need as quickly as possible."

"Right this way, sir."

"She didn't like the red pajamas?" I asked as he followed me to the other side of the store.

"She said red was too bright and wanted an exchange." He handed me the brown bag.

I searched in the drawer beneath the pajamas display, and grabbed a black pair.

He took the pajamas from me and leaned over. "Misty, do we know each other?"

My heart jumped but, before I could say anything, Imogene was suddenly by my side. "Are those more to your liking, sir?" she asked with little tact.

"Maybe," he remarked. "Do you have yellow?"

Now, he didn't seem to be in a hurry.

Imogene said quite curtly, "We have several colors, sir."

"Thank you, Imogene," he said as I pulled the yellow ones from the drawer. "Look, there's one in pink as well." He pointed to the drawer.

"Yes, sir." I laid out a pink pair next to the yellow.

"And purple, too," he exclaimed, looking at Imogene. "Who knew there were so many colors of this style of pajamas?" His voice was kindness itself.

"We also have them in cream, green, and two shades of blue," I remarked, laying these colors next to the pink, wondering when was the last time he'd shopped for women's lingerie.

"Imogene, you've been most helpful. Thank you." He turned, dismissing her.

"Take as long as you need. I'll be near if you need something else," Imogene quipped, turning on her heel. I could feel more than hear her stomping away on the extra-thick carpeted floor.

As she disappeared, he leaned over and whispered, "Is she always so abrupt and… well… rude?"

"She has her moments, sir." Then, I quickly added, "Imogene has been here for twelve years. She reminds us how she started at the store right after high school and knows the stock much better than any other employee."

"Does she?" he asked.

"Oh, yes," I answered truthfully. "She knows every nook and cranny of this place."

He chuckled. "Well, her people skills suck."

I glanced toward the cashier's counter and found Imogene glaring my way. I took a deep breath, suppressing a chuckle.

"Might I suggest the cream-colored ones for your wife?"

He laughed. "They're not for my wife, but my daughter."

I was surprised, yet happy at his answer.

"My daughter just graduated from college and is going off for her masters in August." He mimicked his daughter in a high-pitched twang, "I can't make friends looking like a fire engine." With a soft, low voice, he said, "Black is more subdued."

He laughed and leaned his back against the wall next to the display, crossing his arms over his chest.

"Got it." I put the black pajamas to the side and slowly replaced the other pajamas in the drawer. "Why did you want to look at the other colors?"

He grinned. "Imogene was hassling you. I was determined to have you help me while giving her a reason to leave."

My response was very business-like. "Will this be all, or would you like to take two for her?"

He smiled at me. "I'll take two pairs, please."

"What are her school colors?"

"Red and black."

"Not the University of Georgia, is it?"

He blurted out, "How did you know?"

"Georgia is the dominant university with colors of red and black." I glanced sideways at him, stating proudly, "Besides, I'm an old Georgia Bulldog, myself."

"Good school, I understand."

"The best."

"So, tell me, how did you get out here so far away from home?"

I noticed how Imogene was circling the store, moving our way, so I changed the subject. "Since you are getting her two black pairs of pajamas, I have just the thing for a graduate student in Athens, Georgia." I picked up the pajamas and took him over to the robes, choosing a black one with red trim. "The perfect set for a Bulldog Master's candidate. The robe's on sale and there's only one extra-small left."

He smiled. "Perfect."

He'd noticed Imogene as well, and nodded at her as he followed me through the store to the register.

Imogene hurried around the next aisle, beating us to the cash register. "Misty, why don't you help me pack these items for this polite gentleman."

"Yes, ma'am," I said and took my place next to her behind the counter.

"I'm so glad we could help you find what you wanted, Mister…" her voice trailed off.

"Thank you, Imogene. Misty was a great help."

Imogene stiffened. "I'm sure she was extremely help-ful." Her icy voice was like a freezer as she rang up his items. "Now, wrap these up nice and pretty for the gentle-man," she said to me.

"Yes, ma'am," I remarked sweetly, as I went to work.

He turned to Imogene and told her, "You have a great shop here. Your staff is quite competent, especially Misty."

"Thank you, Mister…" She smiled her plastic smile. "Your name, phone number, and email, sir? You know, so we can add you to our e-mail list."

He ignored her and said before she could finalize his pur-chase, "Here's sixty dollars. Does this cover everything?"

She took his three twenties and gave him the change. No smile. No 'thank you.' No 'hope to see you soon.' Nothing.

I topped off his purchases in the logo bag with the store's signature tissue paper. "Here you go, sir." My smile was warm. "Have a great day."

He shook Imogene's hand. "Marvelous customer ser-vice, Imogene. Marvelous!"

He winked at me and left the store.

Imogene growled when he was gone, "I can't believe he was so difficult, monopolizing so much of your time. I know much more about this place than you do and am more qualified to help. Good riddance I say!" She placed a 'Closed' sign in front of the register. "What was he bab-bling on about?"

"Trying to choose the right pajamas for his daughter."

"His daughter?"

"Yes ma'am."

"Oh, well, Misty, he must be married. I don't know why you flaunted yourself at him."

Ah, there it was, another zing. I just smiled. She was an irritating supervisor, but she was in charge.

I looked at my watch. "I should have taken my lunch ten minutes ago."

Her eyes narrowed and she squinted. "Take it now but remember you have only thirty minutes."

I leaned down under the counter for my purse.

"And get rid of this horrid bag." She forcefully shoved the brown grocery bag into my stomach.

I smiled at her and dropped the brown bag in the garbage receptacle right in front of her under the counter.

I began to hum as I left the store, heading for the food court. As I hurried along, I thought back to the question he asked, *Misty, do we know each other?* Of course, we know each other, Bastard!

"Hello, again." That deep baritone voice came from behind me.

"Hello yourself." I glanced nonchalantly at the man from my past. "Where did you come from?"

"Well, I dropped off my daughter's present in my car and picked up something I left there."

"And then you hurried back to find me?"

"Yeah," he said with a happy look on his face. "I was hoping to see you outside the store."

"Can't imagine why." My answer was short and sweet. I had no time for this guy who didn't remember who I was.

"Where are you going in such a hurry?"

"Lunch," I said, surprised he had waited for me to leave the store, especially since he didn't remember me. "I only have twenty-five…"

"Why don't you let me buy your lunch today?" he asked. "And then you can tell me why you're working as a salesperson instead of teaching like you always wanted to do."

So, he does remember? Who cares? He doesn't even remember my name, or he would have mentioned it.

"It's none of your business what I do." I picked up my step as I walked from him.

He ignored my statement and kept up with me. "I moved here last year and, if I'd known you were here, I would have dropped by."

"Bully for you." I couldn't believe I even responded.

He continued. "I'm over at the army base. Full bird colonel. My mom lives with me and helps with my daughter."

"That's nice."

The food court was just to my right, and I wanted this to stop now.

I stopped, eyeing him. "Thank you for your offer of lunch, but I'm quite capable of buying my own."

"Still very independent, aren't you?" His smile was radiant. "Come on, let me buy you lunch."

"Strangers don't buy me lunch!" I exclaimed.

"But we do know each other, Misty."

"No, we don't," I stammered and walked faster to get away.

If you really knew me, if you really are the man from my past, you would have... but you did call me Misty. We used to mean so much to each other. Now, you're confusing me.

He took my elbow. "Let's see, you want a corned beef sandwich on rye with mayonnaise and no pickle, right? I used to always cringe when you used mayo instead of mustard."

I didn't know what to say. My mind was in a whirl.

He laughed and pulled me in front of the deli counter. He gave the attendant my order and then placed his. Rare roast beef on deli roll, mustard, tomato, lettuce, and two pickles.

Oh, yes, I knew what he would order.

"Two cokes," he added and paid for our lunch. He guided me to a table for two. He pulled out my chair, like the gentleman I remembered, and handed me one of the coke cups. The lunch crowd was talking and wandering about us, but my focus was on the two of us.

"Think back, Misty Marshall," he crooned.

"That's my maiden name," I said. "It's Morales now."

He gave me a big smile and turned sideways. "Here's my profile, Misty Marshall. Think back to Senior English."

I knew who he was yesterday. He was the one who forgot. We were sweethearts once. But that was before he was stationed overseas. That was before he came home with a…

"I know you're Nigel Weiss," I said. No smile. No acknowledgement of our past relationship. No nothing. I was unsure how to handle this moment. I was a bit panicky. He was the one who forgot, not me.

"In the flesh," he declared, babbling like a brook. "Why didn't you say something? I knew you were familiar yesterday. But I was in a hurry, you know, dealing with a lot. It wasn't until last night that I remembered who you were."

"We've both gotten older."

"Yeah, you had long blond hair which you streaked with red Kool-Aid."

"I needed to be like the other girls in my group."

"I remember thinking that no one carried that look off better than you."

"Is that why you first asked me out? My red streak?"

"Yeah," he admitted with a big smile. "I like how you wear your hair now, short and natural."

"Don't you laugh at my gray hair coming in, boy. You're getting gray as well."

"True, true," he noted. "You do look great, Misty. Really great."

"Thanks," I said with a nod of my head. "You look pretty good yourself." Then I added, "But you always looked good, Nige. Handsome captain of the football, basketball, and baseball teams. Destined for greatness."

"Yeah, and it took me until you were sitting next to me in English class to ask you out."

"Why did it take you over two years to ask me?" We'd never discussed the reason why.

He pursed his lips. "You were always hanging around the Banister twins."

I dropped my head and giggled. "You were afraid of Darrell and Destry Banister? They lived next door and we'd known each other since first grade. Their band practiced in our garage because they had a carport, and I was their singer. Plus, the twins had a car, and I didn't. They were my ride to high school every day."

"I know but they told everyone you were their girl."

I shook my head. "You wasted a lot of time waiting, you know."

He was suddenly silent and his face serious. "Yes, I did," he finally said. "I was stupid to wait so long. Then and now."

I ignored his last statement. "But we *did* get together."

He gave a sincere smile. "Yes, we did."

I took another sip of my coke and didn't respond.

The deli attendant called his name, and he picked up our food.

"What happened to us?" he said when he returned to our table.

I picked up my sandwich. "You went overseas and never came back to me. I moved on."

I took a bite of my sandwich, so I didn't have to talk.

"Misty, we wrote back and forth the entire time we were in college. We went out every time we were home." He reached over to take my hand. "I asked you to marry me before I was sent overseas."

"I remember," I moaned and pulled my hand away. "Oh, how I remember. I sang 'Let It Be' over and over again, crying my eyes out."

"Our song." He was silent for a long minute. "We loved each other, didn't we?" His voice cracked and I looked up to see the agony in his face.

"Oh, yes, I loved you deeply, Nige."

"So, what happened?"

"Your sister said you'd married a local over in Bosnia." I reflected on the past. Now, my heart was racing, and my stomach was filled with butterflies. Butterflies? No, more like a million snakes. I was no longer hungry and pushed my sandwich away. "You didn't love me anymore, so why should I continue to write?"

"No, no, that's not what happened."

"I moved on and took a teaching job in Ohio, Nige."

"I heard that when I returned home months later. I wanted to explain everything to you, but you were gone." He sighed. "I married Marta because her father was selling her to the mayor of her village who was in his sixties. Then she was raped by renegade soldiers, got pregnant, and ran away. The only way to save her was to marry her. I did and…"

"I don't want to know what happened, Nige. I stopped loving you a long time ago." I shook my head to snap back to the present. "I received my masters at Ohio State and that's where I met the most marvelous man, Eduardo Morales. I didn't return home after that."

"I know. And then you had three boys, right?"

"Yes," I admitted and then scrunched up my face. "How did you know that?"

"My mom. She's kept me informed of your whereabouts. But she didn't tell me you were here."

"My husband's family lived here so, when he became critically ill a few years ago, he wanted to come home so he could be buried in the same cemetery as his family."

"I'm so sorry, Misty."

His voice sounded heartfelt, but I didn't want to talk about this anymore. It was all I could do to not cry. I looked at my watch.

"Well, it's so good to see you Nige." This time I was able to crack a smile. Not a very good one, I admit. "Thank you for lunch, but I must get back." I stood and pulled my purse on my shoulder, turning to walk away.

"But what about us, Misty?"

I looked back at him. "Us? There is no us, Nige. That died a long time ago."

I started walking back to work, but he was immediately at my side. The next thing I knew, he had taken me into his arms and kissed me.

I was surprised and pushed myself from him, slapping his face. "You're a married man, Nigel Weiss," I sneered. "Don't take those liberties with me!"

"Oh, no you don't," he blurted out. "You're not getting away from me again!" He jerked me towards him and held me tight.

"Give me a break, Nige. Don't embarrass me in front of God and everybody," I chastised him and tried not to cry, but wasn't very successful. "I don't want to be involved with someone who cheats on his wife!"

"You know, I never stopped loving you." He tucked my head under his chin. "I know you never stopped loving me. I can see it in your eyes and the tears you're crying right now."

"But you're married," I sobbed. "Even if I loved you, nothing could be done about it."

He stood back for a moment and wiped tears from my cheeks with his thumbs. "I'm not married, my love."

I sniffled. "Not married?" I wasn't sure I'd heard him correctly.

"No, not at all," he exclaimed. "As soon as Marta had her baby, we divorced, and I got custody of our daughter."

"Your daughter?" I was confused by his comment. "You're raising Marta's daughter as your own?"

"Yes, as a matter of fact," Nige said happily. "She is a wonderful child, well not a child anymore. I've dragged her around the world with me. My mother joined us to help take care of her. She's twenty-two now and ready to be on her own, I hate to admit. Her name is Misty, by the way."

"You named her after me?"

"I told you I loved you since the first day I saw you in high school, remember?"

I grinned.

He kissed me again and this time I returned the kiss. "Last night, when I returned home and realized it was you at the store, I asked my mom for the engagement ring I had picked up when I was in Tel Aviv all those years ago."

My voice was shaking, "Engagement ring?"

"Of course, your engagement ring." He got down on his knee in front of me. "Misty Marshall Morales, will you marry me?" He opened a small box of worn black velvet to show an exquisite diamond ring inside.

"You don't even know me," I whispered.

"Oh yes I do," he chuckled. "We'll work out all the kinks and make everything work."

"What about the children?"

"Misty, our children will love us both when they see we still love each other despite all the years that have passed."

Tears were cascading down my cheeks and I couldn't speak.

"I have to stand, Misty. I'm not as young as I used to be." He laughed and stood up. "My dearest, give me an answer right here before God and everybody."

I smiled at him, nodding my head yes, and he swung me around.

"So, are we going to conquer the world together and sing the Beatles' famous song?"

As he placed the ring on my finger, we both sang the chorus of "Let It Be," just like we did years ago.

Then I asked myself a hard question.

Love was complicated enough when we were young, Now, it's even more complicated. Can two old fogies like us in our early fifties make it together as lovebirds despite all the years we've lost?

As the crowd around us clapped, the man I've loved since high school took my hand and whispered, "I've loved you forever, Misty. Never forget that."

"I didn't realize how much I loved you until right now."

We kissed and I knew the answer to my question.

Oh yes, we're certainly going to try! No matter the complications!

Dancing in the Dark

Sandra Montanino

Rolando wasn't home yet. Angelina slipped into bed and prayed with her hand firmly around the Saint Jude medal Rolando had given her long ago. His last words as he left that morning still echoed in her mind, *A large rush order came into the tobacco shop. There's no way to roll that many cigars in time without my working late into the night.*

It wasn't the day that worried Angelina, but the danger of crimes committed in darkness. She played games and read stories to Donny until bedtime. But that was hours ago.

Now, as she lay in bed, the clock struck 11:00. Rolando said he'd be working late into the night, but how late was *late*? She worried about the possibility of crime after reading news articles about muggings, robberies, and murders at night.

A chill passed through her as she recalled how when she lived in Ybor City with the chaos and terror of Florida's greatest fire. People screamed and ran from the flames, then a gun went off and Angelina froze. The gangster Bettino fell in front of her, feet from where she stood.

She pulled the covers over her to stop the sudden chill thinking of that day. Bettino laid in the street covered in blood, but it was the memory of his eyes that remained vivid. They were dark, wide, wild, and filled with horror as he died staring at a vision in the sky no one else could see.

The Mafia's Nico Trezza terrorized everyone with his gun and one Italian word, *Omerta!* The ultimate threat to murder. *You talk, you die.*

Angelina squeezed her eyes shut to erase the scene from her mind. Most people in Little Italy were good, but there were some bad ones, like Frankie Pantano and his gang from the streets.

Angelina checked the clock again as midnight approached before extinguishing her kerosene lamp and getting into bed. Feeling helpless and well aware that anything can happen in the street, she tossed about until sleep mercifully overtook her.

Quiet enveloped the apartment as another hour slipped by until the key rattled in the lock and dissolved into the stillness. The door opened, followed by a slight rustling sound.

Angelina had always been a light sleeper and stirred a bit when she heard the movement. She slowly opened her eyes and saw her husband's silhouette in the darkened bedroom. "Oh, Rolando, I was so worried. I'm so happy you're home."

"Worried? A stampede of wild zebras couldn't keep me from returning home to you."

Angelina yawned. "Then, I guess, I'm lucky the zoo rounded them all up."

He undressed, slipped into bed, and put his arms around her. "I've been thinking about you all day."

"I've been thinking about you all day, too." She saw no reason to confess all her imagined terrifying scenarios.

Rolando kept his voice low. "Angelina Aguirre, my

wife, I have something to say to you. When our train pulled into New York, I couldn't wait any longer to marry you and start our life together. We had barely set down your suitcase when we said our vows."

"Yes, my suitcase. As I recall, you jumped on the train without one—with nothing."

"Not with nothing. Remember—I had you." He pulled back her hair and kissed her neck. "But there was something else missing from our wedding day—something very important."

Unlike the hesitation she had experienced when she married Fabian Dominguez, her union to Rolando stood out as one of the grandest events of her life, equal only to the birth of her son. Every instant of their wedding service and every word spoken leading to the moment he slipped the gold ring on her finger remained a treasured memory.

"I don't know what you mean. Nothing was missing from our special day, Rolando. Even if our families were not there, it was truly one of the happiest days of my life," she whispered.

"The ring has been with me for two years, waiting for the right time to make you mine. But we've yet to share our first dance. It's a European tradition dating back three hundred years—more or less. And, since both our families came from Europe, we have let everyone down in two nations by breaking this sacred tradition. We have offended all our relatives, those still here and, even worse, those in the hereafter."

Angelina smiled. "Oh, no. How careless of us."

"Yes, it's true. Remember how it rained the day after we married?"

Rolando couldn't see her grin in the dark. "Are you saying our ancestors' tears caused it to rain?"

"It's obvious, isn't it?" He nuzzled against her ear. "We missed one of the most romantic wedding rituals."

Once again, he found a way to touch her heart. Angelina's eyes widened as she listened to Rolando's passionate explanation of how the groom takes his wife in his arms.

"Everyone in the room that's watching seems to disappear while the couple have their first dance," he said.

"If you look at your wedding ring, you might notice we are already married. So, are you suggesting we should get married again and have our first dance?" said Angelina.

"Actually, what happened was just an oversight—a bad memory slip that needs to be fixed. It can't go on like this. I need this dance with my wife."

Rolando still spoke in whispers with his arms around her. Angelina smiled. "While I've been worrying all day and night if you were safe and how I could not withstand the heartbreak if something bad happened to you on your way home. All the while, you've been thinking about dancing with me. Is that right?"

"It's a serious concern. Now, may I have this dance?"

"Now?" she murmured.

"Yes, now."

"There's no music, nowhere to dance, no—" She giggled. "Besides, it's very late."

"*Shh*," said Rolando. "That's why it's perfect." He put his arms underneath her, lifted her out of bed, opened the bedroom door, and carried her into the front room. Angelina's eyes widened in stunned amazement as he gently set her down.

The darkened room glowed with an array of flickering lighted candles, and they took her breath away. "You did all this for one dance?"

"I envisioned this moment all day," said Rolando. "As soon as I walked through the door, I moved the furniture, cleared it for our first dance, and I lit all the candles I bought when I slipped out to eat. One day, when we are old, I want us to remember that on the darkest night, with little Donny asleep in his room, we danced barefoot by candlelight in each other's arms."

"It looks so beautiful, Rolando, and I love you for

even thinking of this."

With intricate shadows swaying around the room, Rolando reached for Angelina's hand as their eyes met.

"I have a confession," said Angelina shyly. "I've never danced with a man, never learned how."

"Well, that's good to hear. It makes it even more special that you have this first dance with the man who truly loves you." Still holding her hand in his, he put his arm around her waist and pulled her close. "Just follow my moves and you'll see how perfect we are together."

Angelina put her free hand on his shoulder.

"I am honored to be your first dance partner, Angelina Aguirre."

"But there's no music."

Barefoot, in their nightclothes, and with only a few strands of moonlight peeking in between the curtains, Rolando softly sang a love song in her ear. He had a beautiful tenor voice and held Angelina close as they drifted around the floor.

Her first few steps were awkward attempts to follow Rolando's lead. However, in his arms, amid the glow of candles, Angelina recognized that dancing together was a language all its own, like his touch and all the beautiful words he spoke about love. He kissed her the moment he felt the shift of how she suddenly relaxed in his arms, as if they were all alone in the universe.

"Love is a wonderful affliction, Angelina. It all started when I caught a glimpse of you for the first time. I think it happens in our minds and without our consent, then startles us because we have nothing to do with it and no control over it. Every action, movement, and thought becomes affected. Suddenly, we've made a connection with all the generations that fell in love before us. Love has a mystical energy, and when we discover it, nothing is the same after that."

"I was never the same after we met again. God has given us another chance. You've made this night magical," said Angelina. "No bride could have ever had a more romantic first dance with her husband."

Angelina realized something amazing about love, it breathes and has a pulse.

"We will dance tonight, tomorrow, and beyond the tomorrows. The life ahead of us is more important than the life behind us, despite the hardships we've faced and the time we've spent apart. So, when we are old and our memories start to fade, we will speak of all the wonders we experienced and what you won't be able to remember, I won't be able to forget," said Rolando.

"I can think of nothing that will remove this beautiful memory of how once, you lifted me out of our bed in the middle of the night while the world slept, and you sang love songs to me as we danced barefoot in the dark by candlelight."

Rolando traced his finger across her cheekbone and over her lips. "There are some things that outlast time because no one can thrill me like you do. Love isn't something, it's everything."

Christmas Cards and Valentines

Renae Weight Mackley

Alisha cleared her throat and began her critique of my English assignment—a personal exchange with a stranger.

Hello, Soldier: Happy Holidays! I hope you get to enjoy some seasonal fun. As for me, I celebrate Christmas. Mom, my younger sister, and I bake cookies and trim the tree. You should smell the kitchen.

"Nice touch. Very domestic," Alisha said.

We attend church services. Do you have services where you are? I'd love to learn more about you but I suppose you must settle for learning about me.

I will be graduating from high school soon and will make the honor roll. Too much competition for high honors.

Alisha turned to stick out her tongue at Brandon at the desk behind her.

"What?" he said, holding up protective hands. There was a glint in his eye and he half smirked as if he had been listening all along. She turned back to face me across the aisle from her.

I love to read and hang out with friends. "Change that to 'voracious reader,'" Alisha suggested. "It sounds sexier."

Brandon tapped Alisha on the shoulder. "Why go for sexier when it's to a soldier she'll never meet?"

She ignored him and read on. *No, I don't have a boyfriend. Yet. Haha. But I have a cat, Alfie, who loves to sprawl on my lap as I read or do homework. I'm thinking of going into teaching.*

Alisha lifted one brow. "You are?"

I shrugged. "Who knows? I just threw that in."

Alisha chuckled.

"What's so funny?" Brandon asked, his dark eyes on her.

"Tessa knows what she's doing, smarty pants. She's adding relatable stuff for our hot student teacher to read. Go back to your own partner."

Her voice was low, but I couldn't help bopping her on the head with my notebook. "Shh."

"Hey." She frowned and went back to reading the card.

I hope this Christmas card finds you well and cheers your day. Thank you for serving. Stay safe. God bless—Tessa Monrich

Later that day when the bus let us off, Brandon elbowed me. "Mr. Chesterfield, huh?" We had to walk half a block to our homes diagonally across the street from one another.

"If you breathe one word to him…" I gave him my crustiest glare. He had the cutest smile even when I wanted to be mad at him.

"He's at least four years older than us."

"So. My parents are six years apart."

"You could just tell him." Brandon lifted a shoulder. "Brutal honesty, y' know? Doesn't seem like Plan A has gotten you anywhere."

Humph. I crossed my arms over my coat. He did have a point.

We walked the remaining steps in silence before parting ways.

I thought about what Brandon had said all week. Getting good marks in English wasn't getting me as noticed as I'd hoped. I just didn't know how to execute Plan B. Anything spoken would certainly not be private. Asking Mr. Chesterfield out would have to be in a note. At the end of the semester, so he wouldn't have the excuse of having me as his student. That gave me two weeks. I composed several notes and finally let Alisha read one, which she approved.

I dug my note out of my backpack with sweaty palms, waiting for the bell to ring so I could get to English as soon as the classroom emptied. Entering, only one person had beaten me there. Mr. Chesterfield stood at the front talking with the teacher, showing him an open jewelry box. *A ring box!* My steps froze and my throat started closing up.

"She'll love it. What a Christmas present!" my teacher said, smiling.

I spun around and raced out the door, bumping into Brandon on the way.

"Tess?"

He'd seen the tears in my eyes. "Contacts." I didn't look back until I'd reached the restroom. I didn't know if I could face him or Alisha asking me questions. I couldn't stand to listen to Mr. Chesterfield telling the class it was his last day and what a great experience he'd had in Honors English. At least he would go to his grave without knowing how I enjoyed the lilt of his voice, the confidence he exuded, the width of his shoulders, the scruff on his chin… Christmas was going to be crappy this year.

It snowed two days after Christmas. Mom sent me and my sister outside 'for some fresh air'. We both complained while donning coats and gloves until she closed the front door behind us. The snow was perfect for building a snowman. We decided on a snowwoman and began rolling balls that practically shaped themselves. The snow was deliciously sticky.

A door across the street shut and Brandon headed to

his mailbox. He had a big wave for us then crouched to check for mail. I couldn't help myself. The snow was too perfect. *Thud.* Heavy, wet icy crystals slid down his coat.

"Hey!" He whipped around. "It's like that, is it?" Those nice teeth appeared as he shaped a snowball in gloveless hands.

If I danced around long enough before he could figure out which spot to throw at, the snowball would be too cold and he would drop it. Instead, he crossed the street, gaining on me, and tossing the ball between his hands. That cute grin turned evil as I slipped from snow onto wet grass. I went down. "No! No fair!"

He loomed over me, his arm cocked back, that stupid smile telling me I was doomed.

"Get her, get her!" my sister chanted.

He squinted at me. "Tessa. You don't wear contacts."

"Brandon. You have scruff."

"It's school break." Then he washed my face with a cold snowball.

Three weeks later as I sat on a bus seat after school, looking out the window, an envelope dropped onto my lap. I looked up to see Brandon passing my seat for a bench in the back. I opened the envelope to see a sheet of notebook paper folded in quarters. I unfolded it to find a large pen-ciled heart taking up the perimeter. Inside the heart, I read these words:

Brutally honest, clean-shaven, cookie-loving male seeks clear-visioned voracious reader to be his valentine.

I blinked and read it again. His courage warmed my thumping heart and a smile spread over my face. When we got off at our bus stop, Brandon's focus remained on his feet, though we were close enough to bump shoulders. His vulnerability tugged at me. I silently reached for his hand and interlaced his fingers with mine.

Cabin-Net Caught Me

Virginia Babcock

Matt focused on keeping his balance on the icy path. His duffel made him top heavy. He reached the cabin door safely, then landed hard on his back as soon as he tried to push the stubborn door open. He lay on his duffel face-up fighting tears.

Matt hated crying. He told himself it was the throbbing pain from landing on the frozen ground—tailbone first. But deep down he knew it was heartbreak. The thought he'd been avoiding all day beat him down at last: "She's gone."

He made it inside the cabin after three attempts to stand. A fire behind the grate warmed the room and improved his outlook. His great-grandpa's hideaway was supposed to house him and Rosalyn on their honeymoon. He pulled her ring from his pocket. Soot marred the gold and diamond.

Matt placed Rosalyn's and his wedding rings in the teacup on the mantle. Behind the cup stood their engagement picture. Grief swamped him. Shock over the freak car accident aggravated his grief. She died coming to their wedding.

* * *

There was a rattle at his door, then it opened. After two weeks alone in the wilderness, he hadn't expected to see anyone, least of all the only other woman he'd ever loved besides Rosalyn: Marley.

She gently pushed him back into the cabin. The door shut, and she pulled him close. His arms rose instinctively.

"Oh, Matt!" Marley's tears cut off her words. Matt was surprised at the relief he felt at having another human near. He'd been solitary in his grief for too long. He clutched Marley tightly as he buried his face against her neck and cried.

Eventually, Matt opened up in a fit of emotional overload. He explained how anxiety over a late bride turned to horror at news of her fiery death, holding her funeral, and how he'd escaped here to grieve. Afterwards, Matt collapsed against Marley.

Marley gently steered Matt to the cabin's bed and tucked him in. Later, he woke to find her in bed with him. She snuggled close and kissed his ear. Instinct, memory, and thoughts of death combined, and they made love. He found peace at last.

Matt woke alone. He was a groom without a bride who'd finally had a wedding night. Confusion reigned, but he felt better until guilt over this overrode his other emotions. Fuzzy thoughts, remnants of a dream filled his head.

He found her note: "See you in 12 months."

Hadn't they connected? Wasn't that why the sex had been so fulfilling?

Matt rubbed his face. Suddenly, he remembered. It was no dream, but a memory. In the night, he'd rolled over and mistaken Marley for Rosalyn.

Marley had yelled, "This is why you should wait a year before remarrying."

She, too, was gone.

He screamed, "What have I done?"

Set Sail With Me

Keyra K. Allred

"Shipping out tomorrow," growled the harsh voice of the large shadow passing the small doorway as the woman sitting sat outside, petulantly sharpening the iron ax head.

"Why bother telling me?" Ljóta grumbled, the scorn in her voice barely reined in. Bullheaded clan chief or no clan chief, the blonde refused to leave even an inch to be taken from her save by brute force.

"You're coming, aren't you?"

The high-pitched whine of stone scraping against metal halted. Ljóta dared not look up, dared not breathe. Fear choked her heart, pushing anticipation back as a warrior faces a defiant horde. Terrified that she had misheard the great bear of a man blocking the sun above her, Ljóta's mind raced. Had the gods struck her down with madness so early in life? Her grip tightened on the oak handle worn smooth by the dreams of a dozen winters. Those winters had come and gone, and every summer brought disappointment. She would never leave the village.

"Don't play with me, Fastúlfr. This ax is plenty sharp to gouge a hole in any of Odin's tricksters, even a burly old king." As often as she'd considered it, Ljóta had never actually threatened her tribe's ruler before. Anxiety had gotten the better of her and she couldn't stop to care. Men had been maimed or killed for less.

"As much fun as it would be to watch you try, you don't want to waste the strength you'll need to row. Seas can be choppy and even your squabbly sapling arms might come in handy on the trip south," Fastúlfr grunted with an infuriating raise of his bushy red brow. "We leave at daybreak," he said dismissively while stomping away.

Ljóta bit her lip, determined to keep her mouth shut and body rigidly still. Blood roared under her skin, thrumming painfully. Her bones ached, pressure swelling, racing from the toes in her boots, up her legs, through her ribcage where her lungs had ceased their continuous pumping of air, and right up to her still furrowed brow where, against every ounce of her Viking training, it twitched.

At last, Fastúlfr's hulking sight disappeared behind the trees and Ljóta exploded from her seat as though filled with Thor's lightning. She saw nothing of her surroundings. Not tree, nor rock, nor small animals jumping from her path, tittering fearfully for the undergrowth. Who needed sight when your feet knew their path better than you know your own face? Ljóta's mind was vibrating with static as after a tremendous thunderstorm. She would not be daunted on her quest.

Hurtling through the open door before she had the notion she had arrived, Ljóta barely stopped before catapulting straight into the woman at the washing barrel. The brunettte's arms were full of the linen cloth she would use to bandage wounded warriors and animals alike. Whipping around, she barely kept a hold on the laundry, which was lucky because having to wash them again would have meant some trouble for the creatures she had waiting for care. Not to mention a boatload of warriors heading out to sea in the morning.

Ljóta stood, gasping in air as she gazed upon her, drinking in the picture of her beloved. Lines at the corner of full lips, deep from the need to constantly smile, giggling when Ljóta could not keep her feet under her and fell flat on her face or behind. Ljóta would gaze up, sheepishly rubbing the sore spot, and Bríet would laugh, music pealing to the top of the mountain, cerulean eyes squinting happily as she wiped tears away. Oh, Bríet. Ljóta loved her so much, breath snatched with each brush of fingertips. Every thought, every glance, every touch, every single stolen moment saturated Ljóta's soul to overflowing and she felt paradise whether Valhalla awaited her or no.

"Well, hello to you, too," Bríet said, carefully placing the linens in a basket to be folded later.

Ljóta's breathing hadn't slowed in the second it had taken for her love to turn around and address her. If anything, her breathing sped up, dazzled as she was by the woman before her. Without another thought or word, Ljóta lunged forward, gathering Bríet up into her arms, embracing with all the love and excitement in her heart.

Bríet let out a squeak of surprise and the dog lazily chewing a deer leg in the corner raised his head in alarm. It didn't last long and he went back to his bone. Bríet's confusion soon abated, and she relaxed into the tight hold of her lover. Burying her face into Bríet's neck, Ljóta inhaled the many scents that always surrounded the woman. The sea, the pine trees, the wildflowers that held on to the beginning of summer, the sweat of working to help others, and that ever-present smell of animal, all mixed into the fragrance of her skin. The fabric of Bríet's dress crinkled under Ljóta's fingertips as she crushed her lover ever tighter and, in her exultation, could only whisper, "It's happening" into her ear.

"What's happening? What's got you so stirred up, my love?"

Ljóta took one last moment to savor the feel of the body wrapped against hers, before pulling back, just enough to look directly into the eyes that captured her soul. Ljóta smiled down at her lover, using a soft touch to tenderly move the tussled hair from Bríet's face.

"I love you," she whispered, lightly. The joy evident in Bríet's eyes added to Ljóta's triumph.

"I love you, too," Bríet replied, leaning in for a kiss more a battle of smiles and teeth. Bríet pulled back, beaming. "Tell me. I know you didn't run up here just to say that."

"I would have, you know," Ljóta replied with a cocky smile. "I would run a thousand miles, for a million years, just to be with you."

Rolling her eyes, Bríet smacked Ljóta on the arm. "But we both know that's not why you're here, oh delectable bootlicker."

Ljóta grinned. She couldn't take it anymore, she had to tell Bríet the great news. "It's happening! I'm finally going!"

"Happening? Going where?" Bríet asked.

"I'm going with the men tomorrow. I'm finally going south!" Her face burned from grinning so widely. Ljóta bounced on her toes so forcefully, she nearly missed the saddened way Bríet dropped her eyes down.

"That's wonderful, my love." Bríet's voice was a shadowed croak of her normal song and Ljóta immediately ceased all movement, confused by the sudden change.

"What happened? What's the matter?"

Bríet shook her head, squeezing her eyes shut as she bit her lips, a sure sign that something was very wrong with the woman. Ljóta's heart crashed through her stomach. "Please, tell me," she begged, grabbing her love by the arms.

The normally happy Bríet, who took everything in stride, collapsed to her knees, covering her face in both hands, body wracked by silent convulsions. The dog let out a sorrowful whine from his corner, his wounded leg not allowing him to comfort the woman.

"Please! Please, Bríet! Tell me. What has happened? Are you ill? Are you hurt? What can I do? What do you need?" Ljóta pleaded, dropping to her knees, fear carving out her core.

The change in Bríet's composure had happened so suddenly, Ljóta was lost, and her tears flowed in earnest. Bríet kept shaking her head, never uttering a single word, breath rasping from her throat in desperate choking gulps. Air was not reaching her lungs and Ljóta wrenched at the fingers covering her face with a maddened stranglehold, though Bríet resisted her. Years of working with stubborn men and animals in pain had given the woman god-like strength, but nothing could compare to Ljóta's anguished grip.

The tracks of Bríet's tears rent the beauty of her face and wrecked Ljóta's soul, like an unskilled mariner on the fog-covered rocks on the north side of the island. This was not her Bríet, her love, her smile, her light in the mind-numbing darkness. This was some desolate creature in the guise of her heart's desire. The sobbing woman on the floor bore no resemblance to the woman she had fallen in love with against all odds and tradition.

With Bríet's arms now wrapped around her ribs as though to hold herself together, Ljóta was free to place her hands on the woman's face. She struggled to radiate tranquility with just her touch, slowing her breathing to a measured inhale and slow exhale. Bríet's skin felt as molten metal before it's poured into the mold to make weapons that sunder the line between life and death.

Laying her forehead to Bríet's, Ljóta continued to breathe deeply, stroking her cheeks with a soothing but firm rhythm. She begged the gods it would be enough to get through to the woman whose face was soaked with salty tears.

"I need you to breathe with me, beautiful. Will you do that for me?" Minutes. Hours. Days. Years swept by in the moments Ljóta knelt clutching at Bríet before the softest whisper of breath took hold in the woman's lungs. Ljóta could not say her heart leapt for joy, but neither was she ungrateful for the hushed change. She would forever mark it as a significant moment in her life journey. Bríet's eyes remained tightly shut, denying Ljóta a glimpse into their eternal depths, so she pressed a kiss to her forehead so gently, it belied the warrior's exterior.

"I'm sorry." The hoarse whisper did not even make a dent in the air of the room, but Ljóta heard it anyway.

"Please. Tell me why," Ljóta whispered back, just as quietly. Only silence was returned to her. "Darling, I would like to know."

"I can't." Bríet's voice was thick with the emotions weighing on her. Ljóta wanted only to take the burden from her.

"I want to understand. You have me and I want to be strong for you. I will stay, holding you like this through the end of the world if that is what you need of me." Ljóta lightly dragged her nose over Bríet's skin, reveling in the familiar smells that surrounded the woman. Slipping her lips close to Bríet's ear, she whispered, "I am here."

Bríet's body shuddered as she threw her arms around Ljóta's body, clutching at her in abject need. Her face found its way into the crook of Ljóta's neck where it fit so perfectly. She often joked, laying together as the dawn wrapped itself across the horizon of the new morning, that they were made of a matching mold.

The tears had mostly ceased, but talking seemed out of the question and Ljóta was worried about what the hard dirt floor was doing to her lover's body and so she carefully placed an arm under her legs and lifted her up. Bríet curled into her body as though she were a kitten searching for warmth and comfort, and Ljóta carried the woman up the stairs into the bedroom. With a little wrangling, she was able to pull back the furs and blankets on the bed with quick one-handed movements, barely jostling Bríet, before placing her down on the mattress. When she tried to pull away, Bríet refused to let go and so she awkwardly slipped in next to her.

"You would think I'd be better at this with as often as I've slept over," Ljóta joked quietly, wiggling to find the best way to not crush the smaller woman while also making sure she was comfortable. She felt Bríet's body soften the tiniest bit, allowing her to pull the blankets over them, snuggling closer.

"You good?" A tiny shrug in response. Ljóta turned her head to place a long kiss to Bríet's forehead and used one hand to begin threading her fingers through her hair. It was a favorite activity and Ljóta dearly hoped it would help Bríet to open up. "How about now?"

Bríet sighed softly and pressed her nose deeper into Ljóta's throat. That was a good sign as far as the warrior was concerned.

Staring at the ceiling, Ljóta smiled contentedly. "Have I ever told you about the first moment I knew I loved you?" she wondered aloud. No answer came, but she knew Bríet was listening now. "I fell into a stream trying to outrun the boys. They were being mean and saying I couldn't jump it. I was a girl and my legs were too short. Okay, what five-year-old doesn't have short legs, I ask you? But they said I couldn't do it, so you know me, of course I was going to do everything in my power to walk away victorious."

That earned Ljóta a quiet snort and she grinned, enjoying the memory.

"Well, I backed up and took a running leap, I soared through the air. Like a bird, I saw myself flying. It was like freedom had come to claim me and my name would ring out in Odin's halls for all time. My glory would reign supreme. It was magnificent. I was magnificent. And then the water rushed up toward me and my dreams of renown slowed to the point of contact where my foot hit that rock and I plummeted into the water to be swept end over end until I came to a stop in the mud right before the most beautiful boots I had ever seen. Rolling onto my back, I peered into the most bewildering eyes I had ever had the fortune to behold." That earned the blonde a smile against her skin and her heart grew happy just knowing she could be here, in this moment.

"By Thor, were those eyes stormy. They gazed down at me from a face full of fury. The trees couldn't soften that anger, and I was so afraid. I could no sooner free Fenrir of his chains than suffer that this fair maiden feel anything other than joy."

"You were being a fool."

"Probably." Ljóta conceded with a shrug. "But, when I looked closer into that beautiful face, I recognized something under the wrath of a thousand demons." That earned her a smack to her shoulder. "Hey, brutality!"

Ljóta could practically feel Bríet rolling her eyes. "Anyway, I gazed in wild wonder at the concern that I could see. No one had ever shown me that before. I didn't really know what to do with it, to be honest, but it warmed me there on that cold, muddy bank." Bríet squeezed her and Ljóta gave her another forehead kiss.

"And then you tried to get up and I had to carry you home where we found you had twisted your ankle and were stuck in bed for days."

"A technicality," Ljóta waved off, "there were far more important things about that day. That was a day that defined the course of my entire life."

"Oh?"

"That was the day I found my purpose. Eventually, I jumped the stream, and all of the others. I learned to fight and move like a true Viking. I have beaten most of the boys since that day and I will keep going on to be better and better, but that is not my reason for being."

At this, Bríet finally, finally, lifted her head to look her in the eyes, confusion battling across her features. Ljóta gently placed one palm, roughened by years of training, against the woman's cheek, imploring her to believe in her words. "That day in the forest, bloodied and bruised, the sound of jeering laughter ringing out through the trees, that was the day that I became yours. Odin will have his champions, but my life has only ever been devoted to being yours."

Without a word, Bríet's tears began anew as she crashed their lips together. The kiss was hard, a clash of lips and then teeth and then tongues, massaging each other, not for dominance, but eagerness to prove the feelings behind it. Eventually, Ljóta forced it to be slower, softer, pouring out her love in waves of tender touch. The hands that had gripped at Bríet at first, now took their time to savor the fabric that covered her skin, the curves of her body, the long hair with just a touch of curl. She wanted to map every inch of Bríet's body, so that nothing could tear it from her mind.

The fire of the kisses slowed to a simmer, the heat more consumed with tender affection than passionate need until they were left nosing along each other's faces and necks, content in the moment to just feel.

"Will you tell me?" Ljóta whispered at last, her lips faintly running over her lover's closed eyelids.

Bríet didn't open them, but instead found her place once again tucked into Ljóta's throat. Pressing a warm kiss to the skin, she hesitated before finally saying, "I am afraid."

Ljóta could have cudgeled herself for not thinking of this sooner, but still she asked, "Of what, my love?"

"I know you want to leave." She said no more.

"Not you. Never you," Ljóta hastened to assure.

"I know that. Or, at least, I think I do," Bríet replied, brows furrowed. "But there is also fear that you will not come back. Mayhap you are lost at sea, or in battle, or perhaps you find that you like the south and wish to remain."

"You would follow me."

"I do not believe that I could do this. At least, not for a long while. You will be gone and I won't know how you fare until the ship returns, if it returns. It's so dangerous. There are no guarantees that you will be safe." Bríet's breathing became choppy again, and Ljóta made soothing noises while combing her fingers through the brunette's hair.

Ljóta stared upward a moment, considering. "Is there any promise I can make that would put your mind at ease?"

"If only there was."

"I could . . . not go."

Bríet pulled back abruptly, leaving Ljóta's skin stinging. "Don't you say that! Don't ever say that!" Her face was a mask of crimson fury.

Anyone else might have drawn back in fear from the fiery woman, but Ljóta knew her lover. She was terrifying ferocity and determined strength, not to be thwarted, but it was all in defense of her fierce love. Bríet gave her all to those around her and never asked for anything in return. It often got her in trouble, but Ljóta would never assign a word less than absolute passion to it, even when it meant that the blonde needed to practically tie Bríet to the bed to recover from sickness brought on by the spring rains. The animals, the villagers, the forest, the gods. Everyone needed the young healer who was brave in the face of the constant and wearying work.

"My love." Ljóta's whispered words breathed over her lover's face and those beautiful eyes once again scrunched to battle the falling tears.

Bríet's balled fists fell against Ljóta's chest. "You have to go. You have to go. You have to go." She repeated the same words over and over, even as Ljóta wrapped Bríet tightly in her arms. Sometimes a little extra pressure helped the brunette when things got to be too much for her to manage.

"I don't."

"You do."

"The men don't need me." The words felt like sand against Ljóta's teeth, but she willed it to be true if that was her destiny.

Bríet sniffled and shook her head, "It's your dream."

"You are the only dream important enough to hold to."

"I love you." With no further argument, Bríet surged forward in a kiss to put volcanos to shame as Ljóta melted into it.

"I am yours," Ljóta gasped, pulling back, eyes fired to will the words into Bríet's soul, "and we are forever."

"I know," the brunette replied, her face soft with love. "I will wait for you."

Was it the heat from the late afternoon sun that sweltered the upper level of the house, or the two women sealing their love in a pact for all time? No answers were given that night as the two lovers said their farewells.

* * *

Well before dawn, Ljóta leaned over the sleeping body of the woman she loved, pressed a final kiss to her cheek, and walked quietly into the darkness. Heart heavy, she gave one last look at the home that had been enough of hers that she felt the slightest twinge of regret. She may never see it again, she thought, as she ran a quick hand over the grizzled head of the dog who trotted a few steps outside to see her off.

"Take care of her," she said. The dog huffed gently before disappearing back inside.

Ljóta didn't bother being quiet as she wandered the path through the forest to her small house. She knew exactly what to pack, spending every year practicing. Just in case.

Now, her chance had come and her heart felt torn. Would Bríet be safe without her? Probably, she thought with a grin. The question was whether or not Ljóta would be alright without the brunette. Furs draped over her shoulders, Ljóta picked up her ax, adjusting her pack, and gave a last look up the hill.

"I'll come back to you." With those words etched into the wind, the blonde began the walk toward the sea.

* * *

"What's this? Playing at being a Viking again, little Ljóta?" yelled Gorm, as he threw a large leather bag onto the longship. Several of the men paused in their preparations to look at her curiously.

Before the woman had more than a chance to open her mouth to retort at one of the bigger idiots who used to torment her growing up, Fastúlfr shouted, "Save your prattling, worm-belly. Let's not have a repeat of last season."

Gorm's face shot from fair to purplish as the other men chuckled. The whole village was aware of Gorm's first time at sea and how it had been spent with him flopped over the side, his face practically skimming the salt water, cursing it and the mothers of all the gods who would have men set out on such wretched ventures. His father had begged the chief to let him try again this season.

Ljóta ignored him and picked up a satchel while the rest of the men got back to work. Trying not to show the nerves that had sprung up suddenly as she realized this was the moment. Her moment. She raised a boot to hop from the gangplank onto the ship when she thought she heard a different sound. Over the incessant squawking of early morning gulls, came a shouting voice. Confused, Ljóta turned away, expecting danger, only to be tackled onto the ship by a crying brunette woman. Her crying brunette woman.

"Bríet?" Ljóta gasped, confusion and worry warring in her. Had Bríet changed her mind? Did she want Ljóta to stay? How would she feel about that? What would Fastúlfr say? Her future as a member of the village and clan flashed through her eyes if she chose to stay. It would not be pretty. But her priority has always been and will always be to Bríet. Ljóta needed her to be safe and happy. For a brief moment, she allowed herself to question whether sailing off to distant lands and battles was as important to her as the loving woman clinging to her now? Ljóta ran her fingers gently over the soft brown hair still messy from sleep.

"Please be safe," Bríet whispered.

Surprised, Ljóta froze. "You don't want me to stay?"

"I want you to be happy."

"You make me happy."

"I know," Bríet said, lifting her face to link their eyes, "but this will also make you happy. I'll be here waiting for you to get back home."

"You are my home."

"Then come back to me."

"You know I will," Ljóta assured her with a kiss, heedless of their surroundings.

"Finally!" roared a voice. The two lovers were startled from their reverie by loud hooting and rugged fists pounding against the ship's railings, speechless as Fastúlfr smiled down on them. Ljóta shuddered at the thought that most of the men in the village had witnessed the emotional exchange when no one was supposed to know about them. She and Bríet had gone to great lengths to conceal their relationship, fearing the consequences of their love. The men continued howling with laughter as the lovers untangled themselves to stand, skin scorched with embarrassment.

"Took you long enough, whelp!" Fastúlfr said, clapping a huge hand on Ljóta's shoulder. "You two aren't subtle. Don't worry about her, Bríet, we'll take good care of your woman. Unless, of course, she goes wandering over the edge of the boat." He gave a wink to the brunette while Ljóta chuffed in annoyance.

"Fastúlfr?" Bríet queried, never having been nervous before the man before.

"Ah, girl," he softly said, sensing the fear in her, "plan the wedding and we'll make good on it soon as we're back."

Bríet gave a gleeful squeal and wrapped her arms around Ljóta's neck, placing enthusiastic kisses over every speck of skin, while the blonde stared at him dumbfounded.

"Alright! Alright!" he finally called out to quell the happy couple. "Get off my boat. Can't get you wedded until we get back and we can't get back before we've left. She'll be fine."

That almost felt like a compliment coming from the man, and Ljóta's head spun. Bríet nodded joyfully as she and the rest of the men laughed loudly.

Ljóta pressed her forehead to her lover's, breathing in the scent of her paradise. "We are forever."

Their lips met in a kiss that was so, so sweet, yet full of passion and promise, each soul reaching out to soothe the other at their temporary parting. For all of their partings were but temporary, a momentary separation, a stepping into another room and back while eternity played on in the background.

With a quiet "I love you" from each of them, Bríet stepped from the boat into the understanding arms of a few of the village wives. With tears and smiles, they waved their loved ones off as the warriors put their oars to the cold water, heading toward locales unknown, sending their thoughts out into the universe for safe returns.

A pair of blue eyes and a pair of green never left each other, even after the early morning fog swallowed the curved tail of the stern. Ljóta spent every moment thinking about the woman with hair the color of fallen oak leaves in autumn waiting for her.

Six months and fourteen days later, they would meet again, and nothing could pry the lovers apart.

Author Bios

Alex Child

Writing has a unique power, and Alex Child is just smart enough to know that he's nowhere near smart enough to accurately describe it. Between working half as hard as he should and twice as hard as required at his day job, he continues pursuing that indescribable emotional swell from relating to a literary character and sharing their experiences. He hopes his story brings you even just a portion of that rush.

Angela Poole

Angela is a wife, mother of three, and recent grandmother to a beautiful little girl. She has been a teacher for twenty years and in her free time she loves writing, crafting, and thrift shopping. She also loves to travel and spend time with her family and friends. She has enjoyed writing for local newspapers and hopes to publish a novel in the near future.

Cray Dimensional

Cray Dimensional began her writing journey with her high school's literary magazine, but she put it aside to cultivate a career in software development. A few years ago, she used writing as a creative outlet to deal with traumatic events without subject-

ing her family to beginner guitar practice. She honed her skills with the assistance of workshops and critques from her writing group. Today, her published works include "Freedom's Song" in Hemelein Publication's anthology Troubadours and the Space Princesses, *"Amore for Life" in* Third Flatiron's anthology After the Gold Rush, *and "Experimenting with the Dance of Death" in* LUW Romance's anthology Love is Complicated. *You can find her works at craydimensional.com.*

Debra Birdwell Winkler

Debra Birdwell Winkler is passionate about sharing her stories. As a former history teacher, Debra weaves historical events into her stories as well as music. Whether publishing short stories, novels, or poems, she excitedly devotes full concentration on writing—her focus, her job, and her joy (second only to her family). Her debut novel Cycle of Coincidence *was released in November 2022. Several of her short stories have been published in Anthologies, like her story* "Never in a Million Years" in Second Chance, *a nonprofit romance anthology, as well as others have been released online. In 2022, she was nominated for the 2022 Best of the Net NonFiction Award.*

Doug Gibson

Doug Gibson lives in Ogden, Utah. He is a retired journalist, who was opinion page editor for the Standard-Examiner. He has short stories and essays published in more than a dozen publications, including Dialogue, the anthology, "Moth and Rust," and the "Tales From the ..." short story collections that include Ogden's Historic 25th Street. Doug maintains two blogs, one on cult films (Plan9Crunch), and the other on his Mormon faith (Culture of Mormonism). He also reviews business taxes for the Internal Revenue Service. Doug and his wife Kati have four children.

Elizabeth Suggs

Elizabeth Suggs is co-owner of the indie publisher Collective Tales Publishing, owner of Editing Mee, and is the author of several stories, two of which were in a podcast and poetry journal. She is the president of two writing groups, one being part of the LUW. She's a book reviewer and popular bookstagramer. When she's not writing or reading, she's playing video/board games or making cookies.

Erin Poche

Erin is the chief writer and editor for the website T1DStrong. Her published work includes a variety of online and print mediums: Tripster.com, Parent Guide News, BDR Publishing, Synergy Magazine, Beyond Type1, and Salt Lake Valley Journals, where she received the Utah Society of Professional Journalism Award for Minority Issues Reporting.As a freelance writer, Erin has written travel articles, biographies, and blog posts. She also completes line editing, developmental book editing, and proofreading for various outlets. When her nose isn't glued to a book, Erin enjoys hiking with her family through the beautiful Cottonwood Canyons near her home and believes all good things are achieved with a light heart.

Jonathan Reddoch

Jonathan is co-owner to Collective Tales Publishing. He is a father, a copy editor, an academic, and a lifelong learner. He rarely dabbles in writing horror but loves to read it and watch it and occasionally live it. He is the associate editor in the anthology.

Keyra K. Allred

Keyra K. Allred, Romance Chapter Co-President and Fundraising Chair of the LUW, is a born and bred reader who has no home, save it be the disgruntled arms of their gingers, Richard and Eustace. They've written a few award-winning short stories for magazines and anthologies and worked as a Utah journalist. Several novels are always in various stages of finished. The dream is to travel the world, play with animals, and write about it.

Mae Thorn

Mae Thorn, also known as Melissa Schack, indulges in the dual thrill of romance and terror, a unique blend reflected in her writing. Specializing in historical romance, fantasy, and horror, she crafts tales featuring strong women and their captivating partners. With three published historical romance novels—Notorious, Dangerous, and Rebellious—her literary journey thrives. Holding degrees in English and Library Science, Mae pursues her MFA in Writing at Lindenwood University. As co-president of the League of Utah Writers Romance Chapter, she actively contributes to the literary community. Residing near Salt Lake City, Utah, she shares her home with cherished companions: cats Church, Shadow Moon, Sabrina, and puppy Whiskey. Explore more at Maethorn.com.

Renae Weight Mackley

Renae Weight Mackley is a mother to six and grandmother to more. She's a bicycle rider, former substitute teacher, musician, seamstress, and home chef. Just don't ask her to remember names with faces. Mackley's latest American Historical Romance project stems from having lived in Virginia: an American Civil War series, featuring a Northern spy and her Southern beau soldier. You can reach her at author.renaemackley@gmail.com or www.facebook.com/RenaeWMackley

Sandra Montanino

Sandra Montanino lived in three different countries by the age of eight. These rich exposures gave her a wealth of appreciation for her own multicultural heritage. Inspired by the life of her Sicilian grandmother, Sandra has won three National and two international awards for her novel The Weight of Salt. The Weight of Betrayal *is the second book in this trilogy and the third installment,* The Weight of War *will be out in late Spring. Originally from Southern California, Sandra has lived in Provo, Utah since 1993. She and her husband Gennaro are high school sweethearts and the parents of five wonderful children and grandparents to seventeen and a big dog who thinks he's a puppy.*

Sara Violet Scully

Sara Violet Scully, formerly Wetmore, is the award-winning author of "The Christmas Script" and "Searching for Your Song." Her work generally explores heavy themes of loss, grief, and heartache. With an MFA from Lindenwood University, she's also an accomplished writer of creative nonfiction and poetry. But, when she's not writing, you can catch her reading smutty books or playing guitar.

Virginia Babcock

Virginia Babcock has always loved romantic fiction, and now writes her own stories of love and life in the real world and beyond. She believes written love should feel real and science fiction should be scary, but it in a good way. Virginia lives in northern Missouri where she works full-time when she's not writing books. Her husband keeps her constantly entertained the rest of the time. She's published six novels and dozens of short stories, mostly contemporary romance, with a bit of Sci-Fi.

Want more?

Check out our current and future anthologies at
www.LUWRomance.Wordpress.com